The h...
as she...

Faine st... ...ing,
wishing— ...g many things!
Then Burk... took a key from his pocket
and unlocked the door, and she asked
foolishly, "Where on earth did you
get that?"

"From the real-estate agent who's
been trying to sell the place for the
past two years." He grinned down at
her. "Would you like it?" he asked.

"Like it!" She stared up at him, totally
bewildered. "But what—"

"There's one condition," he
interrupted. "I go with the house."
And then, after a long frozen silence,
"I'm asking you to marry me, idiot.
Stop looking so appalled. I've never
asked anyone to marry me before; if
you hurt my feelings now, I might
never pluck up the courage again."

ROBYN DONALD

mansion for my love

Harlequin Books

TORONTO • NEW YORK • LOS ANGELES • LONDON
AMSTERDAM • PARIS • SYDNEY • HAMBURG
STOCKHOLM • ATHENS • TOKYO • MILAN

Harlequin Presents first edition February 1983
ISBN 0-373-10567-3

Original hardcover edition published in 1982
by Mills & Boon Limited

CHAPTER ONE

NORMALLY Faine didn't mind the weather, but sometimes it threw up the sort of day which nobody should be expected to endure. Like today. She had woken up to rain, heavy, with the kind of sullen persistence which threatened an eternity of it. Sure enough, when she closed the door of her tiny bedsitter behind her she was drenched before she could put her umbrella up.

Walking up to the library only increased her discomfort. By the time she got there her feet and legs were frozen, her hands purple where they had clenched on the umbrella handle, and her hair had done what it always did in wet weather, turned itself into a heavy mass of corkscrew curls the colour of manuka honey, not red, not gold, but an interesting amber shade somewhere between.

It came as no surprise to find that the central heating had chosen today to go on strike. Heather, her boss, rang up to whisper huskily that she had tonsillitis and wouldn't be in, could Faine please cope as best as she could, then Central rang to say that there had been so many librarians calling in sick that they were finding it difficult to staff all the branches; as Baillie Street was so small could she manage, just for today?

Faine put the telephone receiver down, lifted winged eyebrows in a half-laughing sigh and looked at her watch. Still a few minutes before she had to open. Just time to hop across to get some lunch.

It was still raining pitilessly when she slipped across

the street, but through the downpour her eye was
caught by a brilliant splash of gold outside the florist's
shop.

Daffodils! Impulsively she veered. And crashed
headlong into someone she hadn't even seen.

Which was surprising, for as he steadied her and
grabbed the umbrella wavering in her hand, she
noticed that he was extremely tall, tall enough for her
to have to lift her head as she stammered apologies.
Six feet three or four, and big with it, she thought, but
he moved with the grace and agility of a man perfectly
in control of his body.

'Are you all right?' The voice was deep and incisive;
he was looking at her with irritated impatience as he
held the now folded umbrella towards her.

Belatedly conscious of the fact that she was staring,
Faine nodded, clutching for her self-confidence. 'Yes,
thank you.'

'I suggest that you watch where you're going in
future.'

And with a curt nod he was on his way. Whew! Faine
thought, watching covertly as she bent to pick out two
bunches of daffodils. A car was waiting for him, a
splendid silver-grey thing with that unmistakable air
of conservative opulence owned only by very expensive
vehicles.

She was not normally easily impressed, but the hard
handsome features of the man stuck in her mind
through the subsequent hours. Fortunately the weather
kept all but the most hardy at home, so she wasn't
rushed off her feet, but as Central hadn't managed to
send anyone out she had a long day to get through.

At least the central heating came on again, and towards six o'clock the rain eased, although the low dark

sky promised more. Faine finished shelving a pile of books, trying to ignore the hollow feeling in her stomach. Lunch seemed a long time ago. A pot of yoghurt would keep hunger pangs at bay until she got home. Auckland's rush hour traffic had almost ceased. Surely, she decided, everyone would be at home now preparing for dinner.

Even thinking of food made her ravenous. Mind made up, she pulled the door to behind her and made another sortie across the road, to the dairy this time. Unfortunately there was an incredibly slow woman serving an incredibly foolish man who had about a hundred things to buy. Faine didn't fidget, for that was not her way, but she felt her nerves tighten as she made her way back across the street. Someone outside the library waited, and not too patiently, either.

'Oh!' she exclaimed, startled, as her eyes met the pale, cold gaze of the man she had bumped into that morning.

'According to this timetable, you should be open now.'

He didn't appear to be complaining; indeed there was so little emotion in the cool voice that Faine's hackles rose. Her first instinct was to defend herself, but she ignored it. Although he tipped her off balance she wasn't going to babble apologies like a callow schoolgirl. Taking a deep breath, she unlocked the door and led the way into the library, fusty now with the smell of raincoats and exhaust fumes.

'I'm sorry,' she said calmly. 'Normally we are open.'

He cast her a swift, rapier-sharp glance before turning to survey the room. After a moment he made his way to the shelves which housed the most popular books, thereby surprising her. He did not look like a thriller reader. He looked, she thought with a slight smile at her own fantasy, like a character from a thriller—one of those ones where the hero had the kind of sexual appeal normally attributed only to the more avid Greek gods. Oh yes, he was strictly from fantasy land, this one.

And probably married. He must be thirty at least, and most men, especially gorgeous-looking creatures like this, were well and truly spoken for by then.

He didn't waste time choosing books. Within a couple of minutes he was back at the desk, handing over several of the more luridly covered volumes, his expression remote.

As she ran the computer pen over his card Faine took a surreptitious glance at the name. Burke Harding, and he lived in St Heliers, that fashionable suburb on the Waitemata Harbour. Somewhere in the recesses of her brain his name impinged, but she wasn't given time to track down the faint tug at her memory.

'Thank you,' he said, and for a moment his eyes rested on hers, and there was cool male appreciation in their aquamarine depths before he turned to go.

It wasn't until she was back in her bedsitting room drinking coffee and listening to more rain that she remembered where she had seen his name before. Of course, his photograph had appeared several times in the newspaper, usually in the financial pages but occasionally in that devoted to the social doings of New Zealand's moneyed class.

Burke Harding was a whizz-kid who had appeared on the scene about ten years ago, setting the financial establishment rocking. He had wheeled and dealed a small stake into a multi-million-dollar empire and was now very firmly established amongst the top both in

New Zealand and Australia. He photographed well, too, Faine remembered, recalling several newspaper shots of him adorned with beautiful women, but the printed image was nothing compared to the reality— almost overwhelming. If there had been any softening in that handsome mask she might have noticed a slight flutter in the region of her heart. As it was she had felt the man's impact, but decided now that any attempt to make an impression on him would be rather like trying to take on Mt Everest without a map and oxygen. Only for the foolhardy, in spite of the calm awareness in that final glance.

As her eyes fell on her daffodils, a brilliant note in her room, she grinned. Better forget about him. It was unlikely that she would see him again.

But later, lying in bed, she found herself wondering at that choice of books. Perhaps financial tycoons needed light relief to keep their minds from seizing up, but somehow Burke Harding and escapist literature just didn't seem to go together. He looked too intelligent, she thought drowsily, remembering the hard strength of his bone structure. Sexy with it, too.

It was only by telling herself firmly that he had no place in her mind that she managed to banish him and finally get off to sleep.

The next day was Saturday, as great a contrast to dismal Friday as any could have been. Gone was the rain, swept away by a brisk cold south-westerly, bearing with it a hint of that other New Zealand.

Far to the south the mountains were heavy with their winter burden of snow.

As she pegged her washing on to the clothes line Faine remembered days like this when her parents had been alive, days spent skiiing at Mount Ruapehu. And because it still hurt to think of them, killed so uselessly by terrorist bullets in one of the countries where her diplomat father had been posted, she put them from her mind, giving it entirely to house-cleaning.

It didn't take long. Her room with its bathroom and kitchen in a cupboard was a small but pleasant home. If only it hadn't been built on the downhill side of the house, she thought, as the inevitable stereo upstairs began blaring. Not that Faine objected to classical music, far from it, but she did find the constant repetition of two or three of the more avant-garde composers at about a hundred and sixty decibels wearing. The upstairs tenants were darlings, but they both suffered from a compulsion to play their favourites at top volume and frequently.

'At this rate I'll be deaf by the time I'm forty,' she told her reflection gloomily. A good brisk walk seemed indicated.

Just for a moment she stared into the mirror, wondering what had brought that glint of appreciation into Burke Harding's eyes last night. She knew her face as intimately as she knew her hands, yet she had no idea how the calm, rather placid features appeared to a man. Certainly she was not pretty, nor yet beautiful, but her bones were good and she was the fortunate possessor of skin like thick cream. Her hair was too curly, but the colour was unusual, that honey-amber, and when she lifted dark lashes her eyes with their steady, rather ironic gaze were a clear gold, so unusual that most people did a double-take.

Not Burke Harding, however. His glance had been frankly appreciative, yet there had been no warmth there as he had noted her eyes and the controlled line of her mouth, the firm, rounded chin above the elegant lines of throat and shoulders. A tall girl, she was lucky in that she possessed a grace which made her every movement a pleasure to watch. Her parents had told her so when she had reached five foot six, and there were obviously going to be a few more inches to add to that total. It had been a small compensation for towering over her friends. Dougal had often spoken lyrically of the poetry of her movements, too. But she no longer believed anything that Dougal had told her, because Dougal had said that he loved her, and that had been a lie.

Shivering, she tied a scarf around her head, knotted it at the back of her neck and made for the door. She was over Dougal, had been for three years, but it still hurt, and if she let it happen she could still hear the smug contempt in his voice as he called her clinging and easy, all the hateful adjectives he had used to wound her when he had discovered that her father had used all his salary to live on and that there was nothing for her.

So she didn't let it happen. Instead Faine walked out into the cool blue and gold day, stooping to pat Wolf, the neighbourhood red setter, as she went through her little peeling picket gate.

A window banged, attracting her attention. It was Anna from upstairs.

'Dinner tonight?' she called in her attractively croaky voice, adding as an inducement, 'It's oxtail.'

Faine laughed. Anna kept trying to marry her off, and as her friends and relations formed an enormous network over Auckland and its suburbs she had plenty of prospective suitors to hurl Faine-wards.

'Love to,' she accepted now. 'I've just made some pâté. Would you like to try it?'

'Oh, bliss!' Someone yelled above the music; Anna made a face and a complicated gesture before retiring back into the house, slamming the window down behind her.

The wind blew down the street, cold and cleansing, strong enough to set the branches of the big monkey-apple trees swaying. August was officially the last month of winter, but the gardens shouted that it was spring. Daphne with its spicy, lemon-scented breath held clusters of rosy pink stars up towards the sun, the perfume of freesias and jonquils mingling with that of newly cut grass from someone's front lawn. Flowering cherry trees were cerise clouds in almost every back-yard and on the crab-apple trees down the footpath the buds were swelling.

Faine stuffed her hands into her coat pockets and made her way towards the Domain, long legs moving easily. She would go down to the pond and watch the ducks before having a prowl around the Museum up on its hill above the city.

The pond was murky; Faine wouldn't have put a toe in it, but the ducks obviously didn't care, and the gardens bordering it were pretty. Dark, flame-shaped magnolia flowers were purple against thin silver branches. Behind the post and rail fence camellias bloomed. An old woman with a small child sat on a bench beneath a bare twisty willow, both tossing scraps of bread at a large white duck with orange bill and faded orange legs and a splendidly aloof expression as it ignored their offerings. Faine grinned and walked on to the grass where the ducks were hungrier and more aggressive.

One particularly enterprising drake came right up and lifted its wings at her, its beady eyes hectoring.

'Greedy pig,' Faine told it severely, but she threw a small piece of bread so that it landed just by it.

It bobbed its head in an absurd little jerk and she laughed, the sound soft and very amused. Set in a hollow as it was, the pond was very still. Faine put her hand up and pulled her scarf off, shaking her curls free.

'That's better,' a strange masculine voice said from just behind her. 'Why on earth do you hide it? Hair like curly toffee. Incredible!'

He was laughing at her astonishment, and as she turned came up towards her, his arms propelling the wheelchair, his grin mocking.

'Feeling sorry for me?' he asked when he brought the chair to a halt beside her.

'Well, yes.' It probably wasn't the best thing to say, but Faine rarely lied.

'The truth!' he exclaimed, and acted extreme shock. Even with his face distorted into an expression of immeasurable surprise he was good-looking in an oddly familiar way, dark hair with red lights, pale eyes and high cheekbones giving a faintly Slavic look to a face which was too thin for the breadth of those shoulders.

'You'd be surprised how few people tell you the truth,' he said now, that cynical grin back. 'Even your nearest and dearest come up with lying platitudes.'

'Perhaps they've tried the truth and disliked your reaction to it,' Faine remarked, dropping another crust in front of her importunate drake.

'Ouch!' He moved his shoulders, narrowing his eyes

at her. 'You're probably right. Why are you ignoring his wife? Look at her, trembling over there, her beak watering as she watches her lord and master scoff the lot.'

'You give her some.' Faine handed over the paper bag.

'Thanks.' He took aim, dropping the crust neatly one inch from the duck's beak. 'How's that, then?'

'Very good.'

He flicked her a taunting glance. 'Well, I may be a cripple, but I'm still capable of a few things.'

Faine lifted her brows. 'Naturally,' she said, and he grinned, a bright challenge.

'O.K., O.K., you've made your point. Don't you ever feel self-pity?'

'Feel it? In my time I've wallowed in it, bathed in it.' She laughed, aware that there was a hard, false note in her laughter but unable to prevent it.

'Gets you, doesn't it,' he agreed, and she sat back into the seat, deliberately unclenching the tight fists her hands had become.

'Yes.'

They sat for some moments in a companionable silence until he asked abruptly, 'How tall are you?'

'Five feet eleven.'

'As tall as I was before I copped this lot. You should meet my brother, he tops you by about five inches, and there can't be many of those about.' His voice altered. 'As a matter of fact, you're going to meet him now. And my wife. Here they come.'

And that, of course, was why he had looked familiar, for the man coming towards them was Burke Harding, and the likeness between them was close enough for her subconscious to have made the connection.

'Look good together, don't they?' he remarked now, speaking very evenly. 'Libby used to be a model. What's your name?'

Faine sent him a direct, very level look before saying, 'Faine Hellier.'

'And I'm Gavin Harding.' He grinned and parodied, 'Hold on to your seatbelts, we're in for a rough ride!'

Libby Harding was a beauty in the modern idiom, superbly dressed, but the effect was spoiled by the anxiety of her expression. Her brother-in-law showed no emotion at all on his hard, handsome face, but the pale eyes, so like his brother's, flicked from Gavin's face to Faine's.

'Oh—Gavin!' That was his wife, with a wealth of reproach in the clear, clipped tones.

Gavin shrugged. 'Hello, darling. Meet Faine Hellier. She likes drakes better than ducks. Faine, this is my adored Libby, and my big brother Burke.'

Faine had to keep tight control over her mouth, for the absurd introduction appealed to her lively sense of the ridiculous. Libby Harding shook hands, her very large, very blue eyes worried, setting at nought the smile she bestowed on Faine.

'Faine,' Burke Harding said conversationally, the deep cool voice lingering over the word. 'A pretty name. Unusual, too.'

'I believe it's Anglo-Saxon. If it is, it means joyful.'

He smiled, increasing the sex-appeal rating by a couple of hundred per cent. Faine's heart performed that unusual manoeuvre known as a jump; she had a horrid suspicion that her cheeks were pink and that he was deliberately turning the powerful armament of his charm on to her.

'Is it suitable?' he asked.

Faine shrugged. 'Like everyone, I have my moments.'

'Not last night, however.' Having effectively gained the attention of the other two, Burke said to them, 'Miss Hellier hurtled herself into me yesterday morning and was the librarian at Baillie Street where I got you those books, Gavin.'

So that explained the mystery of the lurid thrillers. Faine smiled politely through the remarks about coincidence and brought them to a halt by saying briskly, 'Well, New Zealand is a tiny country, so this sort of thing happens all the time. Now, if you'll excuse me, I must be away.'

'Nonsense,' Gavin said loudly. 'You must have lunch with us. Don't be put off by Libby's sideways looks, she can't help but be jealous of any lovely girl I chat up.' He smiled into his wife's face as he spoke, but Faine felt a frown pleat her brow. Very definitely there was something wrong here, beyond what might be expected in such a tragic situation. There was too much tension, and that had been a distinctly taunting note in Gavin's voice. It had struck home too, for his wife looked at him with an appeal in her lovely eyes which couldn't be missed.

Faine caught the hard aquamarine of Burke Harding's glance and saw there an expression perilously close to condemnation. Unconsciously her chin lifted. Ignoring him, she said calmly, 'Sorry, but I must go.' The smile she bestowed on them all was impartial. 'Nice to have met you, Mrs Harding, Mr Harding. Goodbye.'

It felt like an escape as she walked quickly up the hill towards the Museum. Heaven knew exactly what was going on in the Harding family, but she wanted

no part of it. Gavin was certainly driven by more than
self-pity and the very natural resentment any man
would feel trapped in such a cruel situation. The circumstances which brought him to a wheelchair had
come back to her now; he had been a racing car driver
who had almost killed himself in an Italian Grand Prix
some years ago.

Presumably he had recovered as much as he was
going to. An appalling prospect for someone like him,
even though he must have appreciated the dangers of
his way of life. But the Gavin Hardings of this world
were always recklessly confident of their immunity
from harm.

It was a thought to ponder over as she climbed the
wide stone steps to stand beneath the pillared portico
of the Museum, turning as always to gloat over the
magnificent panorama which lay before her.

Immediately below was the Cenotaph, bleak in a sea
of concrete surrounded by the sweep of lawns and a
great swathe of deciduous trees further down the hill,
their bare branches grey against the blue waters of the
inner harbour. On the North Shore the volcanic cones
of Mount Victoria and North Head were green
beehives above houses and the Naval dockyard. The
thin length of a channel punctuated by a white lighthouse separated the North Shore from the long forbid-
ding bulk of Rangitoto, thrust from the floor of the
harbour by unimaginable forces during the last few
hundred years.

Beyond the island were the pearl-blue waters of the
Hauraki Gulf, island-scattered, probed by more
peninsulas, Whangaparoa, Coromandel, Takatu. And
grape-blue in the distance, the double peak of Tamahu,
forty miles north on the mainland, the high cliff faces

of Little Barrier, and on the edge of vision, Great
Barrier, the island which sheltered the whole broad
sweep of the gulf and made it the perfect playground
for Aucklanders in their hundreds of thousands.

Faine sighed, a smile curling the corners of her
mouth before she turned and cannoned into the man
behind her.

'Oh!' she exclaimed, and Burke Harding smiled
down at her, speculation and amusement mixed in that
pale glance.

'You do seem to be acquiring a new habit,' he agreed.
'I'm sorry we made you uncomfortable enough to want
to leave so quickly. Have you any particular exhibit
you want to visit here? Or may I buy you a cup of
coffee?'

Faine couldn't help the suspicious lift of her brows,
but it would have been churlish to refuse. Besides, the
Museum coffee shop had delectable cakes, and she had
to admit to being curious. So she nodded, letting him
escort her into the warm, cosy room, basking somewhat
in the reflected glory of being with quite the most
impressive man there. It was amusing to watch the
various ways women signified their appreciation of his
personal magnetism, some with openly flattering
glances, some more discreetly. The few men who were
there seemed to dwindle in size. Rampant masculinity,
Faine thought ironically, wondering just how much
easier it had made his life. Probably made it more
difficult too, she thought. Gavin had seemed curiously
ambivalent in his attitude towards this magnificent
brother of his, a not uncommon reaction when one so
overshadowed the other.

As if guessing the direction of her thought he said
quietly, 'I'm sorry about this morning. Gavin has

moments when he can't bear himself, so he runs away.'

'How?'

'He has a specially modified car.'

She nodded. 'There's no hope for any improvement, I gather.'

'No. He's going to be crippled for the rest of his life.' His voice was calm, but she caught the undernote of pain and said impulsively.

'I'm so sorry. For him, and for his wife.'

'Ah, yes. Libby.' In another man the pause might have been construed as a hesitation, but it merely emphasised his next words. 'I'm afraid he picked you up this morning just to show Libby that he's still capable of pulling a bird.' Those strange eyes watched her from beneath half-lowered lids. 'His words, not mine.'

Faine chuckled. 'The nerve of it! I thought he looked smug as well as—well, smug, when he saw you come along.'

'Smug as well as what?'

Momentarily her teeth caught her bottom lip before she answered, 'He seemed to be angry. It was as though the sight of you hurt him. I suppose he resents the fact that you can still walk while he's confined to the chair.'

There was an odd little silence, then Burke said calmly, 'I'm afraid he does. It makes him extremely difficult to live with; even before the accident he lived on his nerves. Libby has a hard time of it.'

Why should she get the impression that he was very smoothly avoiding something?

'I'm sorry,' she said again, feeling her way. 'Surely as he becomes reconciled to his condition things will be easier for them both?'

'One can but hope so,' he said with an air of finality, as though the subject now bored him. 'Can I get you another cup of coffee?'

'No, thank you.'

She had no intention of seeming to want to hang on to his company, so she rose to her feet, smiling her calm, sensible smile, letting him see that although he was the most stunning man she had ever been with she wasn't bowled over.

'I hope your brother settles down soon,' she said frankly as they walked across the high columned foyer, her voice echoing slightly. 'And thank you for the coffee.'

She expected a non-committal reply and a casual farewell, but he looked around, those strange aquamarine eyes almost startled.

'You know,' he said slowly, 'it's years since I came here.' He looked down at her, a kind of self-mocking amusement in his eyes. 'Would you mind if you acquired a companion for the afternoon?'

Of course he didn't expect her to refuse, but as she acquiesced Faine found herself wondering just how he would have reacted if she had. Probably never had it happen, she thought, hiding a smile as they set off towards the enormous, superbly carved Maori war canoe which dominated the ground floor.

Four hours later she said cheerfully, 'My feet are quite incapable of going any further. Marble floors may be elegant, but they're killers!'

Burke grinned as he stood upright. They had reached the War section and like all men he was intrigued by the aged aeroplanes.

'Shall I carry you?' he suggested, his glance teasing as it swept the length of her body.

Just for a moment her breath caught in her throat. He was making no attempt to hide his interest in her and she reacted sharply to him, her senses keener than they had been since Dougal—but no, she didn't want that to happen again.

'I doubt if you could,' she said, trying for cool amusement. 'In case you hadn't noticed, I'm a big girl.'

'Tall.' Those strange light eyes rested for a tingling moment on the deep curve of her breast, then moved to the narrow waist beneath the belted suede coat. 'Homer had a word for it.'

'Oh yes?' She was suspicious, as much of the glint of mockery in his glance as of the deliberately provocative note in his voice.

He grinned and turned her towards the stairs, his fingers beneath her elbow strong enough to be felt through the suede of her sleeve. 'But I don't know you well enough to judge your reactions to it,' he said blandly. 'Have dinner with me tonight?'

Too fast, she thought, confused and not exactly pleased by the invitation. He was too much—too big, too good-looking, too attractive by half, with that kind of personal magnetism which made every woman within sight give him a second and more often than not a third look.

'I'm sorry,' she said, every bit as blandly as he, 'but not tonight.'

He nodded. 'My loss.'

And she felt a little piqued that he hadn't issued another invitation, piqued enough to refuse his offer of a ride home. At least that would show him that Faine

Hellier wasn't overly impressed by so much sexual charisma, she thought waspishly, knowing she lied. Faine Hellier was strongly attracted, so it was just as well she wasn't likely to be seeing him any more.

Unless he came back to the library.

CHAPTER TWO

'BURKE HARDING?' Anna was suitably impressed. 'Hey, Stu, did you hear that? Faine's had coffee with Burke Harding! Remember when we went to that ball a couple of years ago and he was there with a super-looking woman in the most beautiful dress I've ever seen? Superb! But you know, the most flattering thing she wore was this air of conscious pride; she just knew that every other woman in that room was envying her! Does wonders for a woman's looks, that.'

Faine chuckled. Anna was a pleasant mixture of astringency and kindness. Her habit of playing the stereo too loudly was about the only thing on which Faine could fault her as a neighbour.

'I believe it,' she said drily. 'You should have seen the amount of surreptitious staring that went on in the museum. He is gorgeous, though.'

'Not a good man to fall in love with.' Anna spread pâté on to a cracker, viewing it with rueful pleasure. 'This is delectable! Don't tell me how many calories there are in every teaspoonful. You're a fabulous cook, Faine.'

'Well, thank you. My mama was an expert. As for

Mr Harding, don't worry about me. I'm not stupid enough to fall for him.'

Stu looked up, a trifle puzzled. 'Why not? He sounds a good catch. He's rolling rich, and if he's so slathered with sex-appeal that every woman within fifty yards starts drooling with anticipation, surely that's all to the good? Better than being the sort who sends them screaming! Money and sex-appeal don't usually go together, do they?'

'Very rarely,' Anna told him drily. 'Which is why he's probably more than a little arrogant, certainly spoilt, possibly just the teensiest bit conceited and definitely well aware of his effect on the average female. Not the best bet for a husband.' She sent Faine a wicked grin. 'Ideal for a lover, though!'

Faine laughed, looking at her with affection. 'You know me, Anna, all hung up on virtue.'

'Quite right too,' Stu snorted with unexpected emphasis. Both women looked an enquiry at him, and he shrugged defensively. 'Don't listen to Anna, you know she says things for effect. You stick to your principles, girl.'

Rather touched, Faine said soberly, 'Well, I intend to.' She laughed, adding with sly humour, 'Not that the streets are exactly full of men trying to tempt me from the straight and narrow path. I think I must have a very wholesome look. Or perhaps men aren't keen on Valkyries.'

'Hardly a Valkyrie, you idiot!' Anna was inclined to be indignant. 'I mean, you're tall, but you haven't got long blonde plaits, and although you're not skinny the last thing anybody could call you is overweight! Don't put yourself down.'

Faine shrugged. 'I'd be stupid not to know that my

height is somewhat intimidating.' She looked down the
length of her body, smiling. 'And let's face it, my contours are hardly sylphlike. Burke Harding said that
Homer had a word for it, but he refused to tell me
what it was.'

'He did get personal, didn't he! I can't imagine him
reading Greek, somehow.' Anna sighed, helped herself
to more pâté and said cheerfully, 'Anyway, whatever
you say, you wear your clothes superbly because you're
perfectly in proportion. I wonder how they put that in
Ancient Greek?'

They all laughed, and having demolished the pâté,
began on the next course. The subject of Burke Harding
came up no more.

But although she tried, Faine was unable to put him
out of her mind. Every day at the library she looked
for him to come in, scolding herself for her stupidity
but unable to hide the unbidden hope that he might be
interested enough to bring his brother's books back.

After three weeks she gave it up, telling herself very
sternly that at twenty-three she should be old enough
not to be impressed by sheer physical glamour and a
masterful personality. Those eyes, their aquamarine
depths so curiously cold and cynical, were warning
enough.

In the meantime, and with considerable fanfare,
spring arrived, bringing with it longer days of a warm
kind lushness which set every green thing growing
madly. There was plenty of rain too as the cold winds
from the south gave way to humid northerlies, but for
several days at a time there was a lazy stillness to the
air which hinted at the imminence of summer. The
last game of rugby was played, tennis began, the harbour billowed with yachts and the beaches became

once more filled with people.

One magnificent day, a dream of blue and gold and green, made Faine sigh wistfully as she hurtled out of the door ready to lose the ten minutes or so of her lunch hour it would take to get a pot of yoghurt. She would have loved to be at the beach or walking in the Domain. Instead she had to spend the long warm afternoon handing out books to people who had suddenly become wearisome to her.

When she heard her name she stopped short, just about to step off the footpath.

'Faine!'

It was repeated. Slowly she turned, saw who spoke, and suddenly the day exploded into life and glitter.

'Hello,' she said.

He smiled down at her, the sun gleaming on the dark copper hair, tanned, faultlessly handsome, redeemed from film-star good looks by his strong jaw and ruthless mouth and the cool mockery in the pale eyes as they took in her startled expression.

'Come and have lunch with me,' he said now.

'Oh—I'd love to, but I have to be back in——' she glanced at her watch '——fifty minutes. And I'm not dressed . . .'

He took her elbow and turned her to where the enormous silver monster was parked just up the street. 'Stop fishing for compliments. You look supremely elegant, as I'm sure you're aware. I rather fancied a picnic.'

'A picnic?' She looked up, met the quizzical query in his glance and nodded, suddenly lighthearted—and lightheaded too! 'Sounds lovely.'

The car was incredibly opulent, superb leather upholstery in pale grey and an array of dials more suited to an aeroplane's cockpit.

After a few seconds Faine asked, 'Where are we going?'

'St Paul's Reserve.' Burke slanted a swift sideways glance, 'Any the wiser?'

'No.'

He was teasing her as if they were old friends, his smile intimate, his eyes no longer cold but laughing, and she was afraid of the pleasure this gave her.

'Good. It's not very far.'

Indeed it was only about five minutes' drive away, a tiny grassy patch overlooking the sea and ringed by pohutukawa trees which clambered up the low cliff. Some hundred yards before the waterfront drive swung away from the coastline on a causeway, so that the little bay at the foot of the cliff was untouched. A peach tree flowered half way down and years ago someone had planted a magnolia in the middle of the reserve. Now enormous, it held its pale pink tulips up to the sun, the new green leaves very fragile and bright against the flowers and the sky. Beneath it was a picnic table and benches.

'The grass is too wet to sit on,' he said, opening her door, 'so we'll make use of the table. Wait a moment and I'll get the food.'

It was in a basket, beautifully packed and complete with a bottle of white wine and two glasses.

'Marvellous!' Faine laughed as he eased the cork free. 'Do you do this sort of thing often?'

He smiled down at her. 'Not as often as I'd like.'

Faine never remembered what they had to eat; it all tasted like ambrosia. Beneath them the waters sparkled through the interlacing branches of the pohutukawas and gulls swooped and dived and settled on the grass to watch with eager boot-button eyes for scraps. A train chuffed quietly across the long causeway. The sun was warm on her face; it and the wine combined to make her sleepy.

'This won't do!' she exclaimed, hiding a yawn. 'I have a whole afternoon to get through yet. Perhaps we'd better walk some of this off.'

Burke laughed and got to his feet, holding out a hand with an unconscious command which had her meekly putting hers in it. Warm strong fingers closed over hers. She felt the pleasant sleepiness vanish, swept away by an excitement which fizzed through her veins and nerves.

He was an ideal companion, amusing yet not flippant, his reactions not hackneyed. She liked the fact that he had not teased her by pretending that her sleepiness meant that she was bored in his company. And if, deep down, the practical part of her insisted that it was because he knew that no unattached woman would find him boring, she hid the knowledge. He was certainly not conceited, though that enormous self-assurance could have been a little intimidating in someone who wasn't so pleasant. No wonder he was usually adorned by beautiful women! The effortless charm was almost overpowering.

Hand in hand they walked along the edge of the cliff until they came to the boundary of the little reserve, a rotten picket fence pushed out of line by a row of trees and shrubs, old and gnarled, yet renewed by the magic of the season.

'I wonder what's next door,' said Faine, standing on tiptoe to peer through the tangled mass of greenery. 'Oh—look! Burke, let's go in!'

'How?' He lifted an eyebrow and looked down at

her, neat in a suit of textured knit, the long-sleeved jacket the colour of her hair, the skirt and singlet top several shades paler.

'There's a path.' And there was too, a narrow winding track probably made by children. But she looked doubtfully at his broad shoulders and his city suit, adding, 'No, it's a stupid idea.'

He laughed and gave her a little push. 'Come on—I know that look. Feminine, and as old as Eve. Why the curiosity?'

'You saw the house?' She trailed along behind him, miserable now. At his nod she said quickly, 'I just wanted to have a closer look. It looks—magic, somehow.'

And he'll think you're a half-wit, she told herself as she lowered her head beneath a branch of privet he held up for her.

But he seemed as interested as she was, and when they had finally made their way through the tangle of trees he stood with her in the sun and looked across the newly mown lawn to where the house slept, hung with festoons of lilac wisteria and pink, drowsily scented jasmine.

Clearly empty, for shutters had been nailed over the windows, it was still cared for. Although the gardens had rioted into a glorious free-for-all of colour and form and scent the roof was newly mended and someone had repainted one of the weather-boards which had lost its coating.

'It's old,' said Faine after a moment, speaking softly.

'Very old.' He pulled her gently across the lawn, critically assessing the house. 'Very early Colonial with the Georgian eye for proportion and elegance. Too

severe to be charming, but immensely satisfying to the
eye.' He looked down at her, smiling, and yet there
was something—not calculation, exactly, more like a
speculative question—which made her wonder just
what he was thinking.

Not that she would ever know. He certainly didn't
have an impassive face, but in spite of their short
acquaintance she knew instinctively that his expression
only ever revealed what he wanted it to.

'I wonder why it hasn't found its way into print,' he
said. 'It must be one of the oldest houses in Auckland
and should be well documented. Let's see what else
there is, shall we?'

The colonnade which supported the verandah roof
was wrought iron, slim strong columns above a verandah of wide boards, pitsawn, Burke said. He seemed
to know a lot about building, Faine realised as she
watched him tap and poke and peer, that dark copper
head tilted. She said so, and he looked up from where
he squatted on his haunches and smiled with an irony
she disliked.

'That's how I started off building.' He stood up
and dusted his hands off. Faine had his jacket over her
arm; she watched as the muscles rippled beneath the
fine shirt.

'I believe you,' she told him drily.

He chuckled and reached for his coat. 'Has my stock
gone down or up?'

'Does it make any difference?' She was honestly
bewildered. Not for the world would she have revealed
that for a moment she had been touched by a physical
hunger that frightened her as much as it excited her.
She had had a vision of those muscles beneath her
hands, the strength and driving force in his shoulders

and arms above her, and the vision had made her
cheeks grow warm. Enough was enough! If she was
going to be assailed by erotic emanations from her
subconscious when she was with him then the less she
saw of him the better.

'Does it matter?' she asked, fighting hard to keep
her voice steady.

He shrugged, those cool eyes very shrewd as they
rested on her face. 'I don't know. I do know your
background. Well-bred, carefully brought up, the best
boarding school, with holidays spent in the rarefied
atmosphere of upper diplomatic circles.'

'Did you check up on me?' she asked crisply, hiding
a kind of desolation with anger.

Burke touched her cheek, his smile twisted in mocking understanding. 'No. That's not to say I wouldn't
have, but Gavin mentioned your name at dinner the
other night. One of the guests was a woman called
Philippa Costain. Apparently she went to school with
you.'

'Philippa Costain?' She frowned, moving away so
that she was free from the disturbance his touch
aroused in her blood. 'Oh—Phil Hunt, that would be.'
She laughed. 'I'll bet you got the whole works. She
used to be a darling, but the most enormous gossip.'

'True.' Beneath the cynical amusement his voice was
hard, as though he didn't approve of the Philippa
Costains of this world. 'Your life while you were
growing up was about as far removed from mine as it
could be. I left school at fifteen, worked as a labourer
on several building sites and then went to Australia to
work at Mount Isa.' He smiled, leaning back against
one of the slender columns, his eyes almost hidden by
long dark lashes as he watched her. 'It was a rough

existence, but I did what I wanted to.'

'Which was?'

'Make a pile. Not much, but enough to give me a start.'

Unaware of exactly why he was telling her this, Faine said quietly, 'I don't see all that much difference, except that you had it much harder and deserve more credit for using your brains to get you where you are today.' She hesitated, before adding, 'If that's where you want to be.'

'Exactly,' he said, and leaned forward to catch hold of her hand and pull her towards him. She resisted, but her mind fought her body, and she gave in. Just this once, she promised herself, as she rested her head against his shoulder. It was pleasant to stand there in the sun, pleasant to be in the light, relaxed embrace of a man who was so much taller than she was. Dougal had been exactly her height.

'You're very astute,' he said, his voice deep above her ear. 'Have you ever got what you wanted, Faine?'

She shook her head, aware that of all the stupid things she had done in her time this was about the stupidest. The rising tide of something very close to desire in her made her straighten up—or attempt to. Those deceptively loose arms suddenly hardened into steel bands across her back.

'Don't move,' he said on a note of laughter. 'I promise not to kiss you. Not yet, anyway.' His mouth was against her forehead; she could feel his lips move as he spoke. 'And I promise not to think you easy, if that's what's worrying you. I know the difference between a virtuous woman and one who's promiscuous.'

'I'll bet,' she said, and felt her blush begin deep inside her and heat every bit of skin.

He chuckled. One hand moved up her back, came to rest in the soft curls at her neck. She shivered as he wound one around his finger.

'Do I frighten you?' he asked, and then, 'I'm not promiscuous, Faine. Not exactly virtuous either, but you can trust me not to seduce you.' Another pause, before he added, 'At least, not until I know you much better.'

And he put her away from him, smiling almost blandly as she looked up at him, her expression gravely questioning. For a moment their eyes locked. She thought she saw a bleak determination in the pale depths of his before he bent his head and kissed her lightly. When he lifted his head the only expression that could be read there was a wry self-mockery that made her shiver suddenly.

'What time is it?' she asked, suddenly eager to leave this enchanted spot for the saner, colder atmosphere of the world outside.

Burke glanced at his watch. 'We've fifteen minutes. Let's see what else there is to see.'

The house was bigger than it had appeared to be, a long low bungalow with a clutter of outbuildings and lean-tos at the back which looked ready to disintegrate. Once there had been a kitchen garden, now a wild tangle of docks and thistles and other weeds, and an orchard where old peach and apple trees still blossomed beneath thick coats of grey lichen. A scraggy orange tree scented the still air with a perfume evocative and poignant.

'They need cutting out,' said Burke, and smiled at Faine's indignant outcry. 'Are you sentimental?' he asked, teasing her.

'Very much so.' She turned away from him, aware

now that he was a very dangerous man. Just ahead was a shed, as rickety and leprous as all the others. Glad of the excuse to avoid those penetrating eyes, she pushed a curtain of cobwebs away from a window and peered into the interior.

'Hey!' she called out. 'I've discovered the attendant nymph.'

'Oh, have you?' Burke came up behind her to look over her shoulder and began to chuckle. 'A nymph indeed!

> 'And ne'er did Grecian chisel trace
> 'A nymph, a Naiad or a Grace
> 'Of finer form, or lovelier face!'

'Are you poking fun at her?' Faine felt suffocated by his closeness but managed to keep her voice light and playful. 'Poor nymph! Isn't she lovely? I adore that look of ineffable rectitude! She looks as though someone has just told her a very rude story.'

And indeed the little marble statue wore an expression of horrified yet smug disgust which was irresistible.

'If she will go around half-clothed, she must expect propositions,' Burke observed smoothly. 'I must say, she's a very fetching piece.' He bent, lowering his head to the level of Faine's so that he could see better into the dim interior before saying as he stepped back, 'You need your eyes tested. That's no nymph, my dear, that's Persephone! And from the look on her face I'd say she's just been confronted by the Dark Lord of Hades.'

'No wonder she looks so upset!' Faine moved away from the window.

He smiled. 'Are you like her in objecting to being swept off your feet?'

'I suppose that was the original sweeping-off,' she said drily. 'And yes, I would object. If I remember my Greek myths at all, being swept off her feet was a milder term for rape.'

'He did marry her.'

She looked at him, half angry, half wary. 'And so there was no rape? Naïve, Burke.'

'Perhaps he loved her.'

'So that excuses it?'

He smiled, a nice blend of irony and provocation. 'When you're angry your eyes glow like amber with the sun behind it. And before you get carried away, I'm not an advocate of rape.' He waited until she looked away before adding softly, 'Unless the lady wants it.'

The sun struck gold from her hair as she swung back to face him, annoyed yet exhilarated. 'Oh, you're impossible! What makes you think that any woman would want to be raped? The idea is—it's horrifying!'

Somehow he was very much closer to her than she had realised. Faine went to step backwards, but he caught her by the arms, just above the elbow, and held her, smiling down into her face with all his formidable charm, and yet he was inscrutable, detached as a cat, she thought feverishly. Those pale eyes, the exact colour where blue meets green, were just like cat's eyes, unblinking, cold and compelling.

And the voice, low and deep and roughly smooth. 'Not for every woman,' he was saying. 'Oh, not the violence, not the assault, an act of hatred by a diseased mind. But for a woman who desires ardently and yet is afraid, to have the decision taken from her can be a freedom, not a bondage. Do you believe that, Faine?'

'*No!*' She shook her head fiercely, dispelling the hypnotic combination of voice and eyes and nearness which threatened her command of her senses. 'No, I can't believe that. And I think it's chauvinistic even to suggest it!'

Burke's laughter was soft, almost pleased. He let her go, drawling, 'I'm quite unrepentant. Every man is a chauvinist, however much he wishes to be otherwise. Surely you don't expect anything other than that?'

'I'm not that naïve,' she flashed, and then, catching a glimpse of her watch, 'Oh, *hell*! Burke, I'm due back in five minutes!'

She was two minutes late, and glad of it, for there was no time for any sort of farewell beyond a hasty goodbye and thanks before she hurtled back into the library, conscious of the fact that her cheeks were flushed and her eyes too bright.

'And who,' Heather asked from her vantage point by the window, 'just *who* is that absolutely *fabulous* man? Not to mention the equally fabulous car which can't possibly be a Rolls?'

'It is,' Faine told her, glad that the library was deserted.

'*Well?*'

Faine grimaced and told her.

'Oho!' Only four years older than her assistant, Heather was happily married but with a very appreciative eye for male beauty. 'They're both beautiful, and I hope you know what you're doing.'

'I won't be doing it any more.' Faine's voice was deliberately light, but the just-made resolve gave it a steely undernote.

Heather looked at her quizzically. 'Why? Don't you like the man?'

'I don't know.' Picking up a pile of books to be shelved, Faine frowned. 'He's not the sort of person you get to know easily. On the surface he's immensely charming, considerate—the ideal companion.'

'But you can't help thinking that to get where he is, there must be rather less pleasant character traits hidden not too far below that charming surface?'

Faine nodded. 'Exactly. It's as though all the charm is a mask to hide the ruthlessness beneath.'

'Ruthlessness is not necessarily a bad thing.' Heather looked cynical. 'Sometimes it's a good thing. Sentimentality and foolishness have probably caused more trouble in the troublesome history of our human race than honest implacability.'

'You're probably right.' Faine remembered that Burke had called her sentimental and wondered whether he despised her for it. 'On the other hand, it's a pretty uncomfortable thing to have to live with.'

'Thinking of living with it?'

Faine stared at her, then closed her eyes as colour rushed from her throat to her brow. 'I hope that wasn't a Freudian slip,' she groaned. '*No*, of course I'm not! I'm not the sort of woman tycoons drape with diamonds in return for their favours!'

'How do you know till you try it?' Heather laughed. 'Oh, you do shock easily. If you could see your face! Never mind, my dear, if you've decided not to see the man again the question's academic, isn't it? Before I forget, Mrs Tulloch wants you to ring her. She said something about dinner.'

Faine smiled, put her pile of books on the central console and dialled a number. 'She invited me to dinner on Saturday night. I'll bet she's going to tell me that she'll have to change the date. It certainly won't be the first time. She's very sweet, but hopeless at dates!'

Sure enough, that was it. Faine agreed to an alternative, chatted for several minutes, then put the receiver down. 'She's just discovered that she's been invited to a wedding on Saturday.'

'They must be riotous occasions, your dinner dates with her.'

'Oh, she's lonely. And I enjoy her company. She goes to a lot of trouble, and we have most interesting talks about the old days.'

'You have a heart like soft butter,' Heather told her, smiling affectionately.

And she could be right at that. Thinking about the way Burke Harding made her feel, Faine wondered gloomily if she was a pushover in every respect. It took a considerable amount of self-control to banish his image from her mind, but she managed it, until she got home and Anna came in through the door bearing flowers wrapped in the distinctive green striped paper of one of the most creative florists in Auckland.

'These,' she said importantly, 'are for you. They arrived an hour ago.'

Even before the card with its initials appeared Faine knew who had sent her the exquisite double freesias, lemon-scented, the thick-petalled flowers as exotic as gardenias.

'B.W.H.,' Anna breathed over her shoulder. 'Faine! Oh, aren't they gorgeous? You lucky thing, you.' Her expression registered lively curiosity and a determination not to give in to it.

Torn between pleasure with the flowers and annoyance at the curtness of the message on the card, Faine smiled reluctantly. 'We went out to lunch,' she said. 'I wonder if he sends such expensive thanks-yous to all his lunch dates.'

'Hardly. He must be trying to fix his interest.'

Faine managed to laugh at her companion's worldy-wise tone. 'I doubt it,' she returned drily, arranging the blooms in a fine glass goblet, one of the few pieces left from her parents' home, 'It was a charming thought, however.'

'You'll have to tell him so the next time you see him.'

Anna was fishing, but Faine knew it was done with the best of intentions, so she smiled with gentle irony, saying coolly, 'I won't be seeing him again.'

Anna's mouth opened, then was firmly closed before she said, 'Your decision, of course, and probably a wise one. Are you making coffee?'

'Yes. Have one with me?'

They spoke no more of Burke Harding, but before Anna left she eyed the freesias once more, as if doubtful of their significence. And several times during the evening when the fresh haunting scent drifted across her nostrils, Faine looked up from the book she was reading and wondered just why he had sent the beauti-ful things. He was too experienced not to know that she was affected by his vivid magnetism; she had seen the awareness in his eyes. Indeed, it had been the main reason why she had made the decision not to see him again.

She had spoken the truth when she told Heather that women like her were not chosen by tycoons as mistresses. It was unfashionable to be a virgin, but she had never met a man who had been able to persuade her to override the principles so carefully instilled in her by her mother. Dougal had come close to it. Her fists clenched as she recalled his caresses and pleading protestations of undying love and desire. False, all of them. Oh, he had wanted her, but his love had been a lie. The only thing which had stopped her self-respect from shattering completely when they parted was the knowledge that she had not permitted him that final consummation. She had wanted to be virgin on her wedding day, to wear her mother's white wedding dress without feeling a fraud.

Since then there had been other men whose kisses were pleasant without being anything more. Until Burke Harding, who possessed the same sort of sensual power as Dougal, only to a far greater degree, there had been no one who could make her pulse run faster.

Dangerous, she thought, stretching in the armchair. She put her book down on the table beside it, hooked her legs beneath her and rested her chin in her hand, elbow on the arm of the chair. More dangerous than Dougal who had been a young girl's love, a teaser, a charmer, shallow and greedy, with a vicious tongue when her stricken eyes had made him feel guilty.

Burke was different. Complex, she decided, remembering the strange little discussion beside Persephone's prison. Clever and calculating, yet with a rare ability to smile at himself, he gave the appearance of being supremely tolerant, but some instinct warned her that he was no easy-going hedonist, intent only on self-gratification. He had too much strength of character.

It wasn't fair for a man to be so good-looking and have with it the charisma and strength of character which marked him as a leader. She frowned slightly, her expression remote, wondering just what sort of childhood he could remember. Certainly not one like hers, privileged, cocooned in her parents' love. If he had had to leave school at fifteen then it must have been because he had to earn his living as soon as was legally possible, which meant a poor home, in this country where poverty was barely known.

Yet he spoke without an accent, his command of the language as good as hers. Which, she thought wryly, didn't say much for her five years' secondary education and the three years at university which had followed.

It was not only his speech which intrigued her. He wore his clothes with the casual elegance of a man who is accustomed to the best. There was certainly nothing of the expensive, ostentatious trendiness which many newly-wealthy people affected.

The idea of Burke being trendy made her chuckle. No, trendiness was not for someone of his height and muscularity. The physical strength he had developed as a builder's labourer was still there beneath the well-cut clothes. She shivered, her skin prickling at the memory of his hands on her arms; he had held her gently enough, but she had not resisted because instinct warned her that those long strong fingers could tighten and bruise. There would be few women who would try to break free from his grip. He had that air of power held firmly leashed, of strength in reserve which automatically made everyone who came into contact with him wary.

And you, she told herself scornfully, are thinking too much about him. It was difficult to banish him, but she would have to try.

CHAPTER THREE

By and large she succeeded. Anna produced a cousin, Greg Horne by name, who had a yacht which he raced with a hard bitten, amusing crew. He was attracted to Faine and said so, but beneath the bonhomie and endearing brashness there was sensitivity and consideration. He was content to let her set the pace. And he enjoyed taking her out on his yacht, he and his crew deriving immense amusement from her complete lack of even the most basic knowledge of yachts and yachting.

'Faine, no one could be that thick!' he protested one evening at the Yacht Club. 'I mean, you've got a degree! How can you possibly not see how the yacht gets from A to B?'

She looked rather guiltily at the bar whereon an array of matches, straws and cigarette packets formed a diagram. 'I just don't see it,' she said, firmly removing her drink from his grasp as he prepared to use it to explain the point further. 'I'm very sorry, but I refuse to believe that wind from the side——'

'Abeam, damn it, girl, abeam——'

'Abeam, then, can push the yacht forward.' She grinned as he clutched his dark head in a gesture of mock despair. '*I* think it's magic—like electricity and television.'

He gave a great shout of laughter and kissed her cheek, swinging her round to face the rest of the crew who had been eager participants in the exercise. 'O.K., boys, let the lady stick to her theories. Behind that cool expression is a brain of purest fluff.'

'And you are a chauvinist of the very worst sort,' she told him, smiling, then went as white as paper. Burke Harding had just walked in and across the room his eyes met hers, cool, deliberate, flicking from her face to Greg's and then back to her.

He came towards her and every other man in the room seemed to dwindle and shrink, even Greg who was asking her if she felt sick.

'No,' she said numbly, terrified by the strength of her reaction, and then Burke was in front of her.

'Faine,' he said coolly, and bent and kissed her cheek as though he had the right.

Greg still had his arm about her shoulder. She felt it tighten in a spasm of rejection before Burke stepped back; somehow she summoned up the strength to introduce him. He stayed for some minutes chatting. He obviously knew what he was talking about. Something he said made them all laugh, and one of the crew told him of Faine's total inability to grasp even the most basic tenet of sailing. He smiled, made a teasing remark which left his eyes remarkably cold and then nodded, said a few pleasant words and walked across to join a group who had just come in.

'Well, well,' Greg said softly, but although there were comments about Burke he said nothing more until they were dancing. And then it was just, 'I didn't know you knew Burke Harding.'

That kiss on the cheek rankled. It had been an intimate little gesture; only she and he knew that it was meaningless. Because of it Faine couldn't tell Greg the truth. Instead she shrugged lightly. 'Not terribly well.'

'The man was possessive,' he said with calm persistence. 'He didn't like seeing you with me. And you looked as though someone had hit you one in the stomach when he walked into the room.'

Faine lifted her brows at him. 'I've been out to lunch with him once. Satisfied?'

He shook his head, smiling wryly. 'No, but I know when I'm trespassing.' He lifted a hand to her cheek, his touch lingering against the smooth flushed skin. 'If you've any sense you'll stick with me,' he said deliberately. 'Harding's reputation with women is not the best. Although I must admit he seems to have quietened down recently. The one with him tonight is a model.'

And totally besotted, Faine saw from one swift comprehensive glance. The girl in Burke's arms was elegantly thin, her blonde hair a mass of frizzy curls, her beautiful face enraptured as they circled the floor.

'I've seen her,' she said. 'Lovely, isn't she?'

Greg smiled. 'Too thin for me, but she certainly complements him. Is that red hair any indication of his temper?'

Faine's shoulders lifted. 'I don't know. He was perfectly charming for the few hours I've spent in his company, but I'd imagine that he could hit the roof if he wanted to.'

'If he wanted to? Hitting the roof is usually an entirely involuntary reaction.'

For a moment Faine felt a quick cold shiver across her skin. In a voice which seemed remote she said, 'Ah, but I doubt if there's ever a time when Burke Harding isn't in full control of his emotions and reactions.'

Followed an odd little silence before Greg looked

down at her with a half smile. 'Well, that's a profound statement about the man from someone who knows him so little.'

'That's how he strikes me,' she parried, and even managed to produce a casual smile to go with her words.

Not that it fooled Greg at all; there was a wry perception in his glance. Although he didn't understand the situation he knew that somehow Burke Harding affected her powerfully.

The evening should have been pleasant. It was well organised, everyone was determined to enjoy themselves, Faine knew that she looked well in a honey-coloured silk dress printed with tiny gold birds in flight. A little more formal than many but not quite as formal as some, she thought, allowing her eyes to roam the room. They came to rest on Burke's model, who was madly trendy in white satin Nehru pants and blouson top, silver slippers and pearl buttons.

Nicely middle of the road. The story of Faine Hellier's life. She grimaced and caught Burke's eyes, quizzical, amused, ironic as he came across the big room, threading his way through the dancers with lithe grace.

For the life of her she could not drag her eyes away. It was infuriating, but she sat at the table beside Greg and watched, unable to avert her eyes, as Burke walked towards her.

Several minutes later she was in his arms, oddly breathless, her skin suddenly sensitive to the slightest pressure of his hands and body. The music was slow, sensuous yet far from sentimental, its clever beat revealing its rock origins. Burke held her loosely, but when they moved she felt the hard length of his thigh against her and the swift tightening of his grip on her hand and across her back. Beneath her fingers the muscles of his shoulders were rock-hard. She found herself wondering what sport kept him in such superb trim.

'Your boy-friend is not exactly pleased,' he observed after a few moments. 'Has he reason to be so possessive?'

A small ironic smile curved her lips. 'His words exactly,' she replied smoothly. 'And the answer is the same for both of you. No.'

'No?' He sounded amused, his voice very deep, his breath warm across her ear. 'A liberated lady, then.'

'If by that you mean am I in charge of my own life, then yes, I suppose I am.'

'Happy?'

She seemed to be spending a fair amount of this evening shrugging, but she did it again, forcing a note of briskness into her voice to cover the sudden wariness she felt. 'Of course.'

He nodded. 'Somehow I can't imagine you and Horne having overmuch in common.'

Faine lifted an eyebrow at him, wondering just what went on behind the handsome mask of his features. 'And you didn't think that you and I had much in common either. Just what sort of person do you think I am?'

'I don't know.' He held her gaze for just too long before dropping his to her mouth. 'I don't know,' he said again rather more softly, 'but I think I'm going to enjoy finding out.'

It sounded almost like a threat. Indeed, when she looked up at him again he met her eyes with steel behind the cynical tolerance, and the smile that tilted the well-cut mouth had very little humour in it.

Faine stiffened, then forced herself to relax. 'That,' she said lightly, 'sounds ominous. How is your brother?'

'As well as can be expected. Still frustrated, still taking it out on those around him.'

She nodded, remembering the taut expression worn by Libby Harding. 'Poor things,' she said softly. 'What an appalling situation for them.'

'For everyone.' Burke spoke crisply, almost angrily, adding at her surprised glance, 'I'm fond of them both. And my grandmother, who lives with us, is devoted to him. I'm afraid Gavin doesn't care who he hurts provided he can rid himself of some of his spleen. Libby comes in for most of it, of course, but the rest of us get it quite impartially, too.'

'He'll end up by killing your affection so that all there is left is loyalty,' Faine said sadly, and wondered why the muscle beneath her hand tensed momentarily.

'That could happen,' was all that he said, delivered in his driest tone before he tightened the arm behind her back, bringing her into gentle but intimate contact with the full length of his body. Faine flinched, but his arm was like a steel bar behind her. When she tilted her head back to look angrily up at him his expression was bland, the only warning a glitter from behind his lashes.

'Dancing,' she said between her teeth, 'doesn't give you the right to—to——' She flushed, angry with herself for being embarrassed, angrier with him for putting her in this situation.

'To hold you this closely?' he mocked. 'Surely that's the object of the exercise?'

'Not in my case.'

'Then why dance with me?'

She turned her head away, pink and tense. He was too sophisticated to force her hard against him, but her unusual receptivity to his nearness made her over-conscious of him; she could feel every movement of every muscle, it seemed, and her response was electric. His hand across her back moved slightly, caressing the skin beneath her dress, his chin touched her cheek, his breath was warm across her skin. To an onlooker they must appear to be dancing in a perfectly conventional manner. Only she knew that her nostrils were filled with the faint masculine scent of him, that every nerve end in her body was vividly, painfully alert and responsive, that as he swung her into a turn for a second or so her body lay against his and she was visited by erotic imagery of such explicit frankness that the flush on her cheeks intensified and spread.

'Why?' he asked again, the soft word a taunt.

'Because I couldn't think of any way to refuse you,' she snapped, furious with him. He knew exactly what she was feeling. He was too experienced not to know what the sudden dampness of her skin meant, and it didn't need the lazy note of mockery in his voice to tell her that he was amused by her reactions.

'I'm disappointed. How easy it is to be mistaken! I had you pinpointed as being extremely resourceful.'

Almost Faine ground her teeth, but common sense came to her aid. It was no use flaring up at him; he would lift an eyebrow at her and make her feel a gauche fool.

Very sweetly she murmured, 'Ah, but that upbringing you know so much about ensured that I have exquisite manners. My mother truly believed that the only thing which prevented complete chaos was courtesy. So you see, although I could have refused to dance with you I have this very strong complex about causing people pain, which prevented me from doing so. I know how fragile the male ego is.'

She lifted her head and gave him a smile, totally false but none the less dazzling.

His laughter widened her eyes until she at last gave in to that charm which he knew so well how to use.

'Cat,' he said with great appreciation. 'Yes, that's better. When you're amused your eyes gleam like topazes and you have an enchanting way of lowering your lashes which is as provocative as it's unconscious. Would your boy-friend object if I kissed you?'

'I don't know, but I certainly would,' she retorted crisply, closing her mind to the frisson of anticipation along her nerves.

'You're probably right. I'll wait for a more auspicious occasion.'

Fortunately the music stopped then and as they found themselves beside Greg and his partner she contented herself with a swift, angry glance at Burke before greeting the others with some relief.

During the rest of the evening he didn't come near her again, but his presence in the room was enough to make her uneasy so that the warm glow of her gaiety had an artificial quality to it.

At last at her door, she tilted her face for Greg's kiss, closing her eyes. He made no move towards her, waiting so long that she lifted her lashes in some bewilderment. Always before he had been enthusiastic enough, although accepting her rebuffal of anything but a kiss with the good humour which characterised him.

'What is it?' she asked.

'Nothing.'

He bent his head and kissed her, gently at first, and then, as she responded, with a fierceness which reached some primitive part deep within her.

It was he who called a halt, breathing harshly, his rugged good looks clamped into an expression of desire which faded almost immediately as he regained self-control.

'I don't like being used as a substitute,' he said thickly.

'What?' Faine was genuinely bewildered.

'You heard. It wasn't me you were kissing. At a guess I'd say it was Harding.' His finger lifted her chin so that her face was open to his scrutiny. A wry smile touched his lips. 'And now you know it too,' he said gently. 'Get him out of your system, Faine. Offering others what you'd like to give him is asking for trouble. I'm not at all sure that it isn't an insult.'

He obviously meant her to smile, and she did, but palely. 'I didn't—I don't——' Stammering, sick at heart, she lowered her head, resting it against his shoulder.

'You don't know, do you?' He took her hands and pushed her away, gently yet with a deliberation she couldn't resist. 'Tall girls like you aren't supposed to rouse protective instincts, but you certainly do. In me, anyway. I'm on the verge of falling in love with you, Faine, and as I'm no masochist I'm calling a halt, right here and now. You may not have been in Harding's company much, but it was long enough for something pretty basic to happen. To both of you, if I'm any judge. Have an affair with him, girl, let him break your heart and get over it, and then I'll try my luck with you. Until then—goodbye.' He kissed her forehead. 'I'll see you around.'

Once inside her tiny hall Faine pushed the door to
and leaned against it, the paint cool against her forehead. Greg had made her feel cheap and very humble,
and the feeling was so unpleasant that it was yet another thing to chalk up against Burke Harding.

Slowly, with movements that dragged, she removed
her make-up and clothes and pulled her dressing gown
around her. Although she was tired she knew she
wouldn't sleep. In her cupboard of a kitchen she turned
the element on to heat some milk. As she waited her
eyes wandered around the little alcove and the room
beyond, almost as if she was seeing them for the first
time.

Like hundreds of other bedsitters in Auckland, she
supposed, except that she was luckier than most and
could afford one with its own bathroom. It had been
unfurnished, so she had been able to mask the prevailing ordinariness with furniture of her own choice, an
elegant modern sofa which opened out to be her bed, a
faded Persian rug, heart-stoppingly expensive but
which she had never regretted buying, and a long glass
and brass table. The walls were painted off-white with
a faint cream tinge and against them she had put prints
and plants, a ferocious Polynesian mask and a wall-
hanging in natural wools.

Eclectic, she had been told her taste was, and she
knew the description to be correct. The room looked
bigger than it really was and far from being almost a
basement. The prevailing atmosphere was one of light,
calm elegance on a fairly slender budget. Much of the
work she had done herself, accepting Anna's loan of a
sewing machine to make the curtains of pale green
synthetic velvet and the cushions in greens and golds

and yellows on the sofa. Many of the accessories which gave the room such an individual air had been found in dingy second-hand shops or at auctions where their condition made them cheap. She had spent hours polishing and restoring them.

Sighing, she poured hot milk into a china mug, washed the saucepan and put it away before going across to the sofa. It hid its other self very effectively. All that she needed to do was pull it out and there was her bed, made up except for the pillows and the duvet hidden away during the day in the wardrobe. It took only a moment to get them, then she put a record on the stereo, a fifteenth birthday present from her parents, and climbed beneath the covers, listening, with a concentration which helped keep other thoughts at bay, to a golden tenor sing melting arias from grand opera.

Hardly a suitable choice, she thought wryly. Not tonight. Tonight she should have chosen Vivaldi or Bach or Haydn, anything but this most intensely romantic music redolent of passion and unrequited love.

The telephone's shrill summons startled her so much that she almost spilt her milk. For a moment she stared at it, dark brows contracted. It was almost two o'clock in the morning. She had never been bothered by callers with weird hang-ups, but she had heard stories. Slowly her hand reached out and lifted the receiver.

'Hello,' she said uncommunicatively.

'Ah, I hoped you'd be at home.' Burke's voice was too familiar, the elusive note of mockery very pronounced. 'I didn't wake you up, did I?'

'No. No, you didn't wake me.' She closed her eyes, fighting the treacherous warmth that suffused her skin.

'What on earth do you want?'

There was no way you could hear a smile, but she knew he smiled before answering blandly, 'Just to ask you to dinner tomorrow night. Actually, it will be tonight, won't it?'

She hesitated. Now was the time to make it clear that she wanted nothing more to do with him. The tenor had been joined by a baritone as they embarked on Bizet's ravishing 'In the Depths of the Temple'. The voices blended in soaring lyricism, thrilling and sending sensuous shivers across her heated skin.

'Yes,' she said, almost inaudibly.

'Yes, it will be tonight, or yes, you will come?'

'Yes, I'll come.'

'Good. I'll pick you up at six-thirty. Where do you live?'

She gave him the address, wondering if she had taken leave of her senses.

'See you then.' A pause, and then he said softly, 'Oh, Faine?'

'Yes?'

'Send him home soon.'

And he hung up, leaving her staring with bewilderment at the receiver. What on earth did he mean?

As realisation struck her she flushed scarlet, fiercely slamming the handpiece back on to the cradle. The complete nerve of the man! Clearly he thought she had Greg there and equally clearly he'd just ordered her to get rid of him. Feverishly she grabbed for the directory, but there were eight B. Hardings there and she didn't know his address, so she was unable to ring him up and tell him to take his nasty insinuations to hell with him.

Morning, of course, brought saner counsel; far too

late. Faine washed her clothes and hung them out to dry, joined Anna and Stu in a post-winter attack on the thistles and weeds which the warm spring weather had encouraged to grow to enormous heights in the flower beds, then spent a pleasant half hour on the verandah in the sun deciding what seeds to plant where, to give the place summer colour.

After that she washed her hair and blow-dried it before using up an hour deciding what clothes to wear. As she had no idea where they were going the choice was made awkward. From bitter experience she knew that in Auckland very few restaurants were open on Sunday. So presumably they were to dine at his home. Perhaps. She didn't know just what sort of style Burke kept at home, and she wasn't helped by the fact that she was wishing fiercely that she hadn't ever got herself into this situation.

Finally she decided on a perfectly plain dress with long cuffed sleeves and narrow front and back yokes from which the skirt fell softly and without interruptions to the hem. The only elaboration was the material, a wide border print of smoky green emphasised by a charging black panther. Dramatic, but saved from gaudiness by the perfectly plain cream background and the simple lines of the dress. With it she wore black shoes and jet ear-rings which had been her great-grandmother's in the days when jet was fashionable.

Once ready she sat down and tried to read. Outside the sun still shone brightly. Daylight saving had arrived on the scene some weeks ago during a patch of unseasonably cold weather. It was warmer now, but the evenings were cool enough to require a wrap of some sort. Faine's eyes drifted from the book to the padded silk jacket flung over the back of a chair.

An intolerable restlessness assailed her. She resisted the desire to leap to her feet and dust every surface in sight. Leaning back on the sofa, she began consciously to relax, working from her toes upwards, taking deep, even breaths.

So intense was her concentration that the knock on her door made her jump, her book slipping from her lap to the rug. She bent to pick it up, stood still for a moment then walked across the room and down the tiny hall to the door, fatalistically aware that in opening it to Burke she was opening it to a future over which she had little or no control.

CHAPTER FOUR

HE was leaning against the porch, twirling a carnation, tawny-gold and enormous, in his hand. When Faine opened the door he straightened up and smiled down at her, those green-blue eyes sweeping the length of her body in one swift, all-encompassing glance before resting for a long moment on the softness of her mouth.

'You look charming,' he said, and gave her the carnation. 'My grandmother sent you this. She said you sounded like carnations.'

Startled, Faine held it beneath her nose. 'I hope that's a compliment,' she said as she stood back to let him in. 'Mm, what a fabulous scent! So many of these hybridised flowers have lost their perfume.'

'Not my grandmother's.'

He dwarfed the flat, as she had known he would. Two enormous people, she thought frivolously as she asked him if he'd like a drink, knowing that she was wrong. She was tall, yes, very tall for a woman, but although her shoulders were wide and her legs were long she was slim and graceful. And Burke moved like a wild animal, with an unstudied litheness which made nothing of his size and rock-hard strength.

'No, thank you,' he said, and smiled as she blinked. 'I don't want a drink. Is that the jacket you intend to wear?'

She nodded, but held out her hand as he picked it up. 'It's too hot yet. I'll carry it for now.'

She was behaving like an adolescent on her first date, only just able to control the unevenness of her voice. Taking a deep breath, she poked the carnation into a vase of cottage pinks which it immediately over-shadowed, and picked up her bag.

'I'm ready,' she said.

He looked around the room and then at her. 'Very nice, but I think I'd prefer you in our Georgian ruin.'

'Oh, so would I,' she said lightly. 'But let's face it, I'd prefer me in many another place. Still, this is better than a lot. I have privacy and it's convenient to the library and to the city.' His closeness was beginning to fret at her nerves. 'Shall we go?'

'Certainly.'

He was not driving the silver Rolls, but the car wait-ing outside was almost as luxurious, the pale green upholstery redolent with that special leather smell. Faine smiled at him as he set it in motion.

'Where are we going, or is it to be a surprise?'

'Didn't I tell you?' he said, knowing perfectly well

that he hadn't. 'At home with my grandmother. A very quiet evening.'

'I thought Gavin and his wife lived with you.'

'They do, but they're away this weekend.'

He overtook a car and turned down a road which would lead them to the Waterfront Drive. His voice hadn't changed, and yet it was as though he had slammed a door in her face. *Why?* Faine wondered uneasily. He must feel Gavin's disability acutely if it hurt to speak of him even in passing.

She began to talk, casually, using an ability gained by watching her mother at countless diplomatic functions—a small talent, but it had smoothed many occasions for her. He followed her lead and by the time he pulled up in front of a house overlooking St Helier's Bay, that moment of withdrawal had receded.

The house was not modern but not very old either. Probably it had been built about forty years ago in a more spacious age. There were big panelled doors which led into a wide hall where a splendidly carved staircase curved its way to another storey. Their immediate destination was a small room with French windows facing a paved terrace, half covered in low creeping plants, and beyond it, the Harbour.

And there was Burke's grandmother, tall, seventyish, with shrewd eyes and a pleasant smile. Very definitely not the sweet little old lady of fairy stories, Faine decided as she was introduced to Ellen Guilford. Clearly Burke had inherited her charm and her intelligence as well as that immense self-possession.

'How lovely you look,' her hostess said warmly. 'So many girls nowadays wear such *peculiar* clothes which do nothing at all for them. I often wonder how they'll feel when their children see photographs of them.'

Faine chuckled. 'Probably just as my mother did when I cried with laughter over the clothes she wore when she was young.'

'Which is a tactful way of telling me I'm old-fashioned,' Mrs Guilford observed. 'You are quite correct, of course, my dear; one of the pleasures of old age is passing highly unfavourable comment on the modern world. I find it grows on one!'

But in spite of her comments she proved to be as up-to-date in her outlook as her grandson, and every bit as astute. As the evening unwound Faine discovered that she was enjoying herself enormously, stimulated by two such keen brains into holding her own in the kind of conversation she hadn't had since her university days.

Although Faine learned they had a housekeeper the superb dinner was served by Mrs Guilford. Afterwards they had coffee and liqueurs in a room lined with books and the conversation eddied and flowed to a background of music chosen by Burke—not overly romantic, but the atmosphere was relaxed and Faine felt his shoulder against hers as they sat on the sofa and knew that something was happening to her that had never happened before.

It was a shock when Mrs Guilford rose, announcing her intention of going to bed. A swift glance at her watch revealed to Faine that it was eleven o'clock, so when his grandmother had left the room she turned to Burke and told him that she ought to be on her way, too.

Something gleamed beneath his lashes, but he replied blandly, 'Of course. You were late to bed last night, weren't you?'

A shaming rush of pink to her cheeks must have

convinced him that Greg had been with her when he had rung last night. For a moment she was poised on the brink of denying it, but she gave a tiny shrug and changed her mind. He had no right to question her about anything!

'I was able to sleep in,' she countered calmly, picking up her bag from the small kauri chest which was used as a side table.

'But not tomorrow?'

'No.'

He draped her jacket across her shoulders. Across the room a mirror above the fireplace reflected them, still as porcelain figurines. The subdued light gleamed on Burke's hair, the colour of beaten copper and turned hers into an amber aureole.

He stood looking down at her, his expression icily remote. Something in their stance, he so watchfully waiting, she with her head bent slightly forward, reminded her of a statue she had once seen, a great beast about to make its killing spring. She looked almost meek, her neck bared for the final, life-destroying blow. A shudder touched her; she moved, and Burke lifted his head and stared across the room at their reflections, and the moment was gone as he said, 'We look good together, don't we? Usually I tower over everyone else.'

Like the model he had escorted the night before, she thought as a pang of pure jealousy tore through her. Aloud she replied drily, 'I know what you mean. And speaking of size—what exactly did the Greeks have a word for?'

He grinned, immediately picking up the reference. A mind like a steel trap, she thought, he obviously forgets nothing.

'The Greeks had a word for almost everything,' he said. 'But this one is *bathykolpos*.'

'And it means?'

His glance roved her face, moved from there to the width of her shoulders and the smooth full curves of her breasts beneath the fine challis of her dress. 'Deep-bosomed,' he said lightly. 'Homer used it. Apparently it was an extremely desirable thing to be if you happened to be a woman in the Heroic Age.'

His hands on her shoulders pulled her into his arms. As they tightened across her back he said into her ear, 'I find that I agree very much with Homer.'

And then he kissed her, his mouth cruel and hard on hers, forcing her head back so that her lips parted. It was an assault, brutal and possessive. He was using his male strength to strike at her femininity. Her hands tightened on his arms as she tried to push herself away, appalled at the savagery he showed. She had thought him sophisticated, too self-possessed to lose command, but there was a bitter hunger in his mouth that frightened her.

It lasted for a moment longer and then Burke lifted his head, muttered something and kissed her again, gently seducing kisses across her bruised mouth until she relaxed, her hands sliding up to clasp his shoulders. He made an indeterminate sound and gathered her in more closely, one hand tangling in the soft cluster of curls at the nape of her neck, teasing her head back so that the smooth arc of her throat was bared to him. His mouth was sensuously sweet as it roved across the silken skin, resting for a long moment on the throbbing pulse as though he enjoyed the feel of her heartbeat beneath his lips.

Faine drew in a ragged breath, caught in the grip of

an excitement totally new to her. Every sense was
heightened so that she could smell the warm, slightly
salty scent of him, feel the smooth covering of skin
under the fine fabric of his shirt, and beneath that the
hard strength of muscle and bone. He breathed deeply
and unevenly and she could hear his heart driving with
heavy insistence into her breast. Slowly she opened
her eyes. His were closed, the dark lashes lying in long
sweeps above the high cheekbones.

A spasm of tenderness caught her with total un-
expectedness. Oh, God, she thought frantically, I could
fall in love with him so easily! And she knew that that
would be the most stupid thing she could do. Whatever
he wanted of her was not undying love; he was far too
wordly to indulge in romantic fantasies.

'Burke,' she said huskily, touching his cheek with
her fingertips.

The long lashes lifted and he looked deep into her
eyes, a searching, penetrating assessment, strangely at
variance with the passion he had shown only a moment
before.

Chilled, almost repelled by the cold speculation he
was unable to hide, Faine pulled away, her expression
cool, only the heat in her skin betraying her.

'We'd better go,' she said, aware of his hands as they
lingered on her shoulders.

He smiled with sardonic amusement and bent his
head to kiss her just below the ear. 'Sensible girl. You're
quite safe, however. I'm hardly likely to seduce you with
my grandmother up the stairs.'

'Do you think you could?' As soon as she said it she
was appalled; it sounded like the cheapest kind of
come-on.

He sent her a long considering look. 'Oh, yes, I think

so. You have a considerable amount of self-control, but the basic warmth is there. So is the basic attraction. We both recognised that immediately.'

'Immediately?'

He smiled and touched her cheek, tracing from her ear to her chin. 'But definitely. All day I remembered that line, and your eyes, like startled topazes above a mouth I knew I was going to enjoy kissing. Why do you think I called in at Baillie Street to get Gavin's books?'

'I don't believe you,' she said, tilting her head to look up into his face. 'You didn't know I worked there.'

'I'd watched you come across the street and I did some checking during the day.'

Almost she was beginning to accept his word, incredible though she found it. A frown wrinkled the smooth line of her brow; she saw quick, cynical amusement in the depths of his eyes and felt a swift shiver of—fear?

'Don't you like the idea of such a determined pursuit?' he asked smoothly. 'You must have realised that coincidences don't happen quite as frequently as they seemed to. Meeting Gavin the next day was a coincidence: nothing else.'

He pulled her against him, holding her gently but with inflexible hands. As he looked down into her astonished face he was smiling, very smooth, very sophisticated, the lean hard features revealing nothing, and yet she knew that beneath that urbane mask he wanted her more than a minute ago when he had purged himself of some dark emotion by kissing her with brutal force. His desire beat against her. Closing her eyes, she turned her head away like someone looking at a furnace when the door is opened.

'Frightened of me?' he asked and, several tones lower. 'I won't hurt you, Faine.'

For all the world as if she was some inexperienced adolescent he was trying to reassure.

He must have seen the swift flash of anger in her glance, for he chuckled and released her, after turning her towards the door. And on the way home he used her tactics from the trip out and spoke quietly, calmly, of nothings.

She didn't ask him in. It was obvious that he didn't expect her to. He listened to her thanks with a slightly bent head and when she had finished he lifted her hand and kissed the inside of her wrist. It was a charming gesture, except that his tongue traced the fine blue vein there in a caress which was so erotic that ever after Faine had no clear recollection of how she had managed to get in through her door. She surfaced standing in her little hallway nursing her hand as if she had hurt it while on the skin moisture dried in a track of fire.

That night she dreamed. It started quite sanely; she was walking down a long corridor lined with mirrors so that everywhere she looked she saw her reflection. Then she realised that each mirror was a door and somehow, in the way of dreams, she knew that people were standing just behind them, listening to her footsteps. She moved on into a wide hall, still mirrored, where people waited silently, all of whom she knew. Dougal was there, and Gavin and Libby, Mrs Guilford, Anna and Stu—everybody she knew, watching as she walked towards them. Burke was waiting too. He had his back to her, but she recognised him, the wide shoulders tapering to narrow hips, the long legs and watchful stance. He swung to meet her, and smiled and put his hand out. She knew a moment's intense joy, then he lifted his other hand to his face, and it was a mask which he pulled away to reveal a death's head.

Although the terror was so real, she knew it must be a dream, but before she could fight free of it she heard laughter and everyone else removed the masks from their faces, and behind each one was a skull, eyeless and grinning.

When she realised that she was awake she lay gasping, her heart pounding remorselessly in her breast while great beads of sweat coalesced on her brow and between her breasts. It was almost dawn, for a bird murmured to itself in the cassia tree outside her window, sleepy little chirps which made the terror of her nightmare recede and begin to fade.

'How stupid,' she whispered, and more strongly, 'How *stupid*!'

But it was not until she had showered and made herself coffee that her equilibrium began to resemble anything like normal. Even then she found the memory of her dream shadowing the warmth of the sun; it was good to get to work and forget herself in the sanity of everyday tasks. It worked, of course; that other nightmare reality faded and was overlaid by the essential mundane reality of the day, but she was glad that Burke didn't come near her for some days until the dream had been swallowed back up by the subconscious from whence it had sprung.

He rang her and that weekend they went to a revival of *Madame Butterfly*. Faine wept at the ending and was teased for her sentimentality, but Burke's mockery was not unkind. Then he took her to a nightclub and they danced until two in the morning. Faine was used to her height attracting attention, but she had never before been the target of so many envious feminine glances. Indeed, when she looked at him herself, her heart swelled. He possessed a rare authority which would have attracted attention even without his height and his superb good looks. They were, she decided dreamily, the icing on a fascinating cake, and she couldn't help wondering just why he had chosen her when there were many other beautiful women with so much more to offer him whom he could have escorted.

For a moment a faint memory of her dream clouded her eyes and she shivered.

'I refuse to believe that you're cold.'

'No.' Why she did it she could never after fathom, but she told him of her dream, only omitting his central part in it.

There was a long silence after she had finished and she tilted her head back to look up into his face, expecting nothing more than mockery. Instead his expression was totally blank, the pale eyes remote and icy. It was hard to tell in the subdued lighting, but it seemed that some of his colour had ebbed away, sharpening and strengthening his features into a merciless mask as he stared above her head.

Faine drew a quick sharp breath. And in a reversal of her dream Burke looked down at her, and the mask cracked and was gone as he smiled at her with warmth and what seemed almost like tenderness.

'Don't look so frightened,' he said softly, and pulled her close, holding her in a gentle captivity as their movements matched, thigh to thigh, his hand warm against her back and fingers, her breasts brushing his chest in a sensual pressure.

Deep within her attraction began to spark into desire, a warmth in her loins that spread through her body with subtle heat.

'Let's go,' he said abruptly, and until they were at her door he was quiet and when he did talk it was with a clipped intonation which was almost curtness.

But at her door he said softly, 'Are you going to ask me in for coffee, Faine?'

She hesitated for a moment, looking at the key in his hand. She knew exactly where such an invitation would lead. He would make love to her and inevitably, because she wanted him with a passion which made her blood run like fire through her body, he would spend the rest of the night in her bed.

It was probably unfashionable to be a virgin at twenty-three, but she was. Neither proud nor ashamed of it, she had had no intention of giving in to the importunities of those men who thought sex after an evening out their right. But this was different, she thought feverishly, and then, only because you want him, you fool.

Aloud she said, wryly, 'No, I'm not.'

Burke inserted the key into her lock. She caught a glint beneath his lashes as he smiled, before he lowered his head, kissed her gently and then not gently at all.

'Just so that you know what you're missing,' he said, that mocking note back in his voice. 'Sleep well.'

If he doesn't get in touch with me again I'll know the exact reason for his interest, she thought drearily as she took her make-up off. Not that he had made any secret of his desire for her; it was there, although never blatant, every time that pale gaze rested on her there was a tiny lick of flame at the back of it, fire beneath the ice like the colour conjured up by the Polar sun from the depths of an iceberg.

Oh yes, he wanted her. But was that all? She had thought—why not be frank and tell the truth?—she had *prayed* that there was more to his pursuit than his desire to take her to bed. Because if that was all there was to it—and she felt an obsessive hunger at the visions that thought aroused—then sooner or later she would capitulate and she would know what it was to lie against him and feel the force of his passion. And later to feel the desolation when he left her, as he would, as he had left other women before her.

That night she didn't dream, but she woke the next morning with an aching head and her pillow was damp.

CHAPTER FIVE

BURKE was waiting for her when she left work the next night. Faine felt a leap of the heart while an intolerable excitement fizzed through her blood. Reining down hard on her emotions, she met the mockery of his smile with a faintly quizzical gleam in the warm depths of her eyes. Thank God for the sort of phlegmatic temperament which made it possible for her to hide the fact that the mere sight of him woke her to a dangerous singing delight!

'You look like spring,' he said softly, his glance sweeping in open assessment over her, lightly clad in a peppermint green blouson dress, soft and romantic with its matching jacket.

Faine smiled, allowing enough disbelief to show him that the flattery was recognised. 'If I remember correctly, she was a redheaded nymph swathed in garlands and very little else. A very ethereal lady. Nobody, with the best will in the world, could call me ethereal.' A glimmer of mischief warmed her glance. 'And you have the red hair.'

He grinned, opening the passenger's door. 'My hair, so I've been informed on the best authority, is copper, not red. And if you think that by referring to Botticelli's nymph you'll coax me into giving you effusive compliments, you've miscalculated.'

The door closed beside her. He swung around the front of the car and got in with the lithe economy of movement she found so attractive.

As he started the engine he turned his head to say blandly, 'You chose that dress you're wearing to enhance every line and curve you possess, and it does it very skilfully. Compliments are superfluous when someone knows herself as well as you do.'

Faine frowned. 'I have the strangest feeling I'm being got at.'

'Nonsense. You're too intelligent not to pick up false flattery.' He smiled sideways at her, his glance resting for a moment on the strong clear line of her profile. 'You have far better taste than most women and you're fortunate in possessing the kind of body that dresses superbly. Whoever had you in charge during your formative years did a good job on you. Most women of your height slump in the hope of hiding away and walk around in flat heels which do nothing for them. Who taught you to be proud of your height, Faine?'

'My mother,' she said softly, more moved by his comment about her mother than by the frank compliment he had given her. 'She was tall herself, about five ten, so she knew what it was like. I was lucky, too, that I didn't grow until I was fifteen, when I had enough maturity to cope with it.'

'At fifteen I was as tall as I am now,' Burke observed laconically.

She had a sudden vision of him, a tall, gangly adolescent, that broad frame not yet filled out, and found herself profoundly moved. Had he been awkward and clumsy, or had he always possessed that easy animal grace? she wondered, and moved uneasily, her hands in her lap suddenly tense.

'Where are we going?' she asked, a husky note deepening her tones.

'To your place so that you can change into something a little less formal and then on to Howick,' he said. 'A couple I know found friends from America on their doorstop last night and have decided to give them a barbecue.'

'Oh.'

She said nothing more, but he stretched out his hand and covered hers in a warm clasp for a second. 'They rang me last night. I did try to contact you then, but there was no reply. I've been in Wellington all day. I could have got my secretary to ring, but I thought you might object to being treated as someone I do business with. I hoped you'd be free.'

He was probably accustomed to having women cancel dates when he rang, but she liked him for not taking her for granted.

'I am,' she said lightly, warmed by his touch and his courtesy. 'Just how informal is this to be?'

He grinned. 'At the Laytons' I've seen everything from a bikini to what appeared to me to be full evening dress. Sal has a genius for hospitality; you'll enjoy her. There'll be swimming too, if you want to.'

In the end Faine chose a khaki jump suit in polyester jersey with a shoulder-baring blouson top and covered it with a knee-length coat in french cotton, the abstract splashes of gold and copper and purple and khaki bringing her hair and skin to vivid, brilliant life.

'Very nice,' Burke drawled as she came through from the bathroom. Obviously he had changed in town, for he wore casual clothes, camel coloured trousers, a fine cotton shirt with a jacket slung on to the back seat of the car. Just what your average millionaire should wear to a barbecue, Faine thought, and then, *Oh God, I love him!*

'Faine?'

She smiled faintly, lowering her lashes so that those too perceptive eyes couldn't see beyond their silky screen.

'What is it?'

For a moment she wondered what he would say if she told him that she had fallen in love with him. It might almost be worth it just to see him disconcerted for once.

'Nothing,' she lied, picking up her bag from the arm of the sofa.

'One day you won't find it so easy to evade my questions,' he told her lightly, without much expression, but there was a glint in his eyes that brought heat to her cheeks.

The Laytons lived in a splendid house overlooking the Gulf, a modern creation of many levels built down a hillside. Mediterranean in style and furnishings, it had an airy, open ambience enhanced by white walls and green plants and a magnificent collection of

modern art in the glowing colours and stark lines of
those New Zealand artists in love with its landscape.

Sal and Philip Layton were as charming as their
home, the American guests were fun, the evening was
mild and mercifully free from insects—everything
conspired to make it an enjoyable occasion. Not that
any woman escorted by Burke could complain of lack
of pleasure. There was nothing to object to about the
lazy possession in his eyes each time he looked at her; he
did not make her uncomfortable. It was just that his
whole attitude stated uncompromisingly that she was
his partner for the evening, and although there were
several unattached men around none of them made any
effort to get to know her.

Flattering, Faine decided, as she met his eyes across
the room. If only she knew what he had in mind for
her!

The pool house was as luxurious as the rest of the
place, each cubicle tiled in blues and greens with one
wall a mirror. Faine found herself in there alone,
having urged her hostess and two other women to go
ahead without her. She stepped into her maillot, clear
yellow and strapless, and thanked heaven for water-
proof make-up. Her hair would dry into riotous curls,
but tonight she wasn't going to care about that. A swift
glance at the mirror showed her that the sleek one-
piece emphasised every good point, from her long legs
to the smooth curves of breasts and shoulders.

Sunbathing over the weekend had given her a warm
glow; not yet a tan, she thought frivolously, but she
looked good.

Vaguely she had heard someone else come in, but it
wasn't until she heard her name that she realised who
they were discussing. And then she froze, unable to

think of any way to reveal her presence without embarrassing them.

'. . . wonder if she's Burke's latest lady,' one said, adding with a little laugh, 'If she is he must have changed his requirements. This one can keep up an intelligent conversation, which is more than can be said for most of his others!'

'Too true. Don always used to say that Burke chose his women for rest and recreation, and that all he wanted of them was a pretty face, a good body and the ability to keep quiet.'

'I don't think that was *all* he wanted,' the first woman laughed meaningly. 'Just who is this one?'

'She's a librarian. Her father was John Hellier—he and his wife were killed when a terrorist bomb exploded in their car in the Middle East. About six years ago, I think. You must remember—there was almost an international incident over it.'

'Oh, the diplomat.' There was a pause before the same woman resumed, 'I wonder if he's thinking of marrying at last. If I remember rightly the Helliers are a good family, one of the original Hawkes Bay settlers. Burke couldn't do better than to marry into that lot— perhaps he wants some background. Not that he needs it!'

Faine bit her lip, furious with herself for allowing this kind of situation to arise. By now she had put faces to the voices and it didn't help matters that she had liked both women, or even that both were prepared to like her.

'Well, he certainly wouldn't have to apologise for her,' the second woman agreed. 'She seems a nice sensible girl and of course she has presence. They make a superb couple, don't they, both so tall.'

'Magnificent. Like lions, all gold and russet and tawny. I'll bet they'd have beautiful children.'

Both women laughed while Faine pressed her hands to her hot cheeks, shaken by an image of Burke's child in her arms.

'Well, for her sake, I hope it's marriage he has in mind,' the first woman observed drily. 'She doesn't give much away, but she doesn't look the sort who sleeps around without any guilt. If Burke wants an affair she's in trouble.'

'She could always say no.'

They laughed together again. 'Would you, if you were young and unattached? Come on, we'd better get into the pool . . .'

Their voices trailed away. Faine took a deep breath as she stepped out of her cubicle, bright-eyed with the heat of her blush still on her skin. Fortunately she managed to get to the side of the pool without either of the women noticing her, but she bit her lip again when her glance picked them out, not yet in the pool. It was stupid to allow herself to get worked up over gossip, not even malicious gossip at that, she thought. The trouble was that their remarks parallelled her own thoughts, reinforcing her conviction that she should find the strength to tell Burke that she didn't want to see him any more.

'Are you going in, or do you plan to decorate the side of the pool for the rest of the evening?' he asked from behind her, making her start and turn her head.

In the half dark he looked too big, the sun's afterglow sliding over his magnificent body in a wash of tawny gold. He lifted a hand and touched her shoulder, running his finger across the satin skin in a shivery caress.

'I don't think I like you like that,' he said, shocking her.

'Oh, why?'

He smiled. 'The old atavistic desire to hide one's woman from all other eyes. You look like the stuff of every man's fantasy—a golden goddess. Into the pool with you before I have to fight them off!'

Her laughter was subdued, a note of mockery hiding the faint touch of hysteria behind it. If only she knew what he planned! Turning away, she brought her arms up and made a creditable entry into the water. For four years she had spent every holiday in a climate where a pool was a necessity, so she was an excellent swimmer. When Burke followed her in it was to find her three feet beneath the surface and almost at the other end, swimming strongly.

'Like an eel,' he muttered when he had hauled her against him. 'Isn't that thing likely to come off?' His eyes moved over her bare shoulders in an intimate glance.

'No. Modern fabrics are marvellous.'

He grinned and let his glance wander down the length of her body. 'I believe you,' he said drily. 'Bad for the blood pressure, however.'

'You're not doing too badly in that line yourself,' she retorted, reaching out with great daring to touch the hard line of muscle down his upper arms.

He drew in a sharp quick breath and when she went to move away held her there by pressing his own hand over hers. Beneath her fingers his skin warmed and tautened; she could feel a muted thunder which must be his heart.

Slowly she lifted her head, shaking it slightly to flick the drops away from her face. His eyes met hers, narrowed and filled with a hard, fierce light that sent a shudder through her.

Then someone called out his name and his hand left hers as he turned, and the moment was over, leaving her shaken and pale, confronted so blatantly with the driving reality of a man's hunger for her.

The moment was over, but its aftermath lingered, making her wary of his touch and his nearness, acutely conscious of the sheer masculine charisma of the man. He knew, of course, and for the rest of the evening the pale eyes mocked her.

The party broke up comparatively early. Jet lag finally caught up with the Americans and as most of those there had families or work to cope with the next day it was only just after eleven when the Porsche pulled away with the hopes of their hostess for a further meeting in the near future still sounding in Faine's ears.

'Enjoy yourself?'

The cool, commonplace enquiry set her hackles up. Very calmly she returned, 'As much as anyone could enjoy a modern tribal initiation ceremony. I liked your friends.'

'They liked you, too.' He sounded indifferent, almost bored.

A car cut in sharply in front of them; Burke slammed on the brakes and took evasive action all in the one moment, his reactions razor-sharp as any primitive hunter's.

After that he was silent, concentrating on the road and probably, Faine thought dismally, irritated by her rudeness.

She leaned her head back, half closing her eyes so that the light from the street lamps shimmered on her lashes. Earlier in the evening there had been a new moon lying on its back in the western sky, but it had set now and the garish city lights effectively blocked out any stars. A small sigh was torn from her. Sometimes she longed almost unbearably for a place in the country, somewhere she could retreat to when the city became too big and too noisy. If one had to live in town there was no better place than Auckland, with its beaches and its parks, two harbours and the great range of the Waitakere Hills on its back doorstep, forested yet crossed by hiking trails, but there were no running streams in Auckland, no morepork to cry in the trees at night, and the stars were hard to see above the profusion of manmade lights.

'That was a sad little sound,' Burke remarked, surprising her. 'Tired?'

'A little.'

'Up late last night?'

'No, not very late.'

Conversation lapsed again until they reached her home. No way was Faine going to invite him in. That exchange in the swimming pool had convinced her that this time there must be no more vacillating. But when he opened her door she allowed herself to be urged into the tiny hall with a kind of fatalistic anger at her inability to say no to him.

'The light switch,' she muttered, reaching out for it.

Those aquamarine eyes must have been able to see in the dark, for he put both hands on her shoulders and turned her to face him. Hard and implacable, his mouth found hers, forcing it open so that he could plunder the sweet depths.

Faine had been kissed before; Burke had kissed her before; and so had quite a few other men. Most of those kisses she had enjoyed. Dougal's kisses had had the power to make her tremble in his arms. But she had never known such intense need as Burke's mouth roused in her now, a crystal flame engulfing her in piercing rapture so that she lost all sense of time and place, her hands clasped tightly behind his shoulders, her face lifted pleadingly to his. So dark ... so dark that she couldn't see anything. There was only the pressure of his mouth on hers, the exquisite sensations he engendered in her as his hands slipped beneath her coat, smoothing across the sensitive skin of her bare shoulders.

When he lifted his head she could have cried out with the loss, temporarily witless as she turned her mouth into the strong warm column of his throat. After a moment she drew a deep breath and began to pull back.

'No!' His voice splintered against her eardrums. 'You don't get away so easily.'

His fingers tightened against her throat, menacing, holding her in a thralldom she was beginning to fear.

'Please,' she breathed huskily, lifting her hands to touch his. 'I bruise very easily.'

'Then stay still.' He spoke with thick arrogance. 'Lift your head—now kiss me again. Not like that,' as she brushed the rough silk of his cheek with her mouth. 'Properly, Faine.'

She should have made a stand for her independence, refused such a peremptory command. But she wanted to feel that incredible tide of sensation again. Slowly, angry with him for making her beg, angry with herself for her capitulation, she tilted her head back and kissed the corner of his mouth, touching the chiselled outline with the very tip of her tongue. She heard his harsh indrawn breath and smiled against his skin, sliding her hands up to rest against the hard line of his cheekbones. Beneath her touch his skin was heated and taut. Strangely, this evidence of his hunger fanned hers into a flame that threatened to engulf her.

'Kiss me,' he muttered fiercely, his hands harsh against the smoothness of her shoulders.

She kissed him then; for a moment the initiative was hers until he took over, punishing her for her unspoken taunt with a ferocity which should have frightened her.

It had exactly the opposite effect. Her desire flared to meet and match his, rocketing beyond all control so that when her coat fell to the floor and his hands pulled the strapless top of her jump suit to her waist she did not protest, although she shuddered as he touched her breasts, the long lean fingers sliding with tormenting gentleness over the soft curves.

'You're beautiful,' he said harshly, holding her when her knees threatened to give way beneath her.

His touch was exquisite, smooth yet with a hint of violence held strictly in check. Faine felt a faint film of dampness cool her heated skin. She turned her head, biting her lip, at the mercy of sensations she had never experienced before. So this was the sweet cruelty of passion, this hunger to experience the ultimate invasion, this mysterious ache in the deepest, most intimate parts of her body.

How long they stood there she did not know, barely aware of anything other than the tantalising movements of his hands and mouth. Afterwards she could never remember unbuttoning his shirt, but the roughness of his chest against the thrust of her nipples made her moan softly and when he stooped to take one in his mouth she gasped with a pleasure almost too great to be borne and slid her arms around his neck, pressing herself against him in a swift movement that revealed only too clearly how aroused she was by his lovemaking.

That Burke was excited too was obvious; his hands moved to her hips and they swayed together, Faine's mouth open against his throat, her whole body unbearably tense with a need so great that she thought she might die with frustration.

And then he put her from him, pulling up her top with a casual expertise as he said, 'No more, Faine. I'm only human, and at this moment my will-power is barely sufficient to keep me in check.'

Shakily, breathing as heavily as though she had just run a marathon, she put out a hand to the wall and leant against it while the tensions he had engendered threatened to explode into a hurricane of frustration.

'Faine?'

Striving desperately to steady her voice, she said, 'It's O.K. I'm just getting my breath back. To invent a cliché, you pack a pretty lethal punch.'

There was amused understanding in his voice. How quickly he had recovered! 'Mm, your response is all that a man could hope for, too.'

Pitch dark though it was, her eyes had become accustomed enough to see a darker form which was him. He bent, and she heard him smother a curse.

'What on earth are you doing?'

'Looking for your coat. Ah . . .' He stood, the coat dangling from his fingers, and put an arm about her shoulders, urging her towards her sitting room. Once inside he switched the light on before dropping the coat on to a chair.

Faine turned her head away, afraid of that keen scrutiny, the hooded assessment which had penetrated her mask right from that first meeting. Not that it would need any great perception to realise what his practised lovemaking had done to her. He had stripped her of every protective skin. Without looking in a mirror she knew that the remains of a flush lay along her cheekbones, that her eyes glittered with a febrile heat and her mouth was full and red. Like an extra skin his touch lay over her, warm, sensual. For the first time in her life she had lost her head completely and now that she was recovering she didn't like the sensation.

'Faine?' There was a hint of laughter in the deep voice, a lazy sexuality that licked along her veins as he turned her to stand in his arms. One hand lifted her chin so that her face was open to his regard.

For a moment there was a naked yearning in her eyes, then her lashes came down to hide it.

'Don't start hating me,' he said crisply, very much the dominant male. 'Or yourself, if it comes to that. Don't tell me no one else has ever made you face the fact that you're a very sexy woman.'

It took all her considerable reserves of strength to say lightly, 'All right then, I won't. You have enough conceit as it is.'

'Indeed?' Burke smiled without much amusement, bent his head and kissed her, painfully. 'Don't look so hurt. If you're deliberately provocative you should be prepared for the consequences. When's your lunch hour tomorrow?'

'One o'clock.'

'I'll pick you up.'

He set her aside and turned to go, leaving her stand-

ing and gaping. The door must have been closed
behind him for at least five minutes before she shook
herself free of her bemusement enough to go down to
it and pull the safety chain across.

Looking back, many months later, Faine supposed
that was really the beginning. After that Burke made a
definite assault on her heart, succeeding so well that
within a few weeks she knew that she was fathoms deep
in love with him, obsessed with him, so drawn to him
that he was the first thing she thought of when she
woke, the last sweet memory before she slept.

Some deep instinct of self-preservation kept her
from revealing the depth of her emotions, helped by
the fact that after that night he never again attempted
to make love to her quite so ardently, contenting himself with a lazily affectionate approach. Faine returned
his light kisses just as lightly, glad because she was
afraid of the suffocating response he evoked from her.
She knew that if he wanted to he could take her to bed
any time and that almost certainly he knew it too.
Hating her own defencelessness, she camouflaged it
with an air of good-humoured sophistication, hoping
fervently that it fooled him.

Several times she dined at his home, but usually they
went out to a restaurant or a night club, to the theatre
or to dine with friends. Amongst them she was
accepted as Burke's latest lover; wryly she thought that
not one of them would believe just how platonic their
relationship really was. She found it hard to believe
herself. One glance at Burke was enough to appreciate
his immense physical charisma, and a further glance at
the tightly-controlled but sensual mouth revealed that
he enjoyed the power his magnetism gave him.
Between them stretched a thread of awareness, fine but

strong, yet although his eyes frequently gleamed with desire he held his appetites under extremely firm discipline.

So those friends were wrong in their summing up of the situation. Not that it made any difference to their attitude to her. They were friendly, a little aloof, perhaps, until they got to know her. Her obvious intelligence came as a surprise to them. Rest and recreation, she thought scornfully, and allowed herself to hope, just a little. But although Burke's friends enjoyed her company there was no possibility of any closer relationship. Always they held back a little. It would not do for any of them to become too friendly with her when they considered a break-up inevitable, and it was Burke who held their regard.

And they were a small circle, a few people whom he had learned he could trust. Faine had been puzzled by his wariness until at a big party she saw him almost inundated by favour-seekers, avid, bored women and those who wanted nothing more than to use his power or money to help themselves.

She felt a profound pity for him then; wasted, of course. He looked down at them with a cold bored contempt, collected her with a glance and left.

'That was—nasty,' she said tentatively as they drove home.

Beside her the broad shoulders lifted in the faintest of shrugs. 'It happens. But you can see why I prefer less public occasions.'

'I can indeed!'

He laughed at the fervour in her voice and took her hand, holding it for a moment beneath his on the wheel before replacing it in her lap. 'You have a soft heart, my dear. I saw the sideways glances of commiseration.

Don't let it worry you. I'm more than capable of dealing with leeches like that.'

His graphic description made her shiver. 'Yes, I saw. A lift of the eyebrow and a curled lip and they turned pale and moved off. Is that how you deal with all importunate hangers-on?'

Unspoken, there was the query: is that what will eventually be my lot? When you tire of me will you freeze me off so effectively that it will be years before I thaw?

Burke was too astute not to know what she meant. 'Not you, my dear, never.'

It should have been comforting, but she was not reassured. A muscle worked in her throat, but she didn't know what to say.

After a moment he continued calmly, 'Not that I can imagine you importuning anyone. You have a cool reserve that I like, the kind of self-restraint that signifies quality. To use my grandmother's terminology, your parents brought you up to be a lady.'

So he had discussed her with his grandmother. Unconsciously her chin came up in a movement not without a delicate arrogance.

His low laughter was maddening. 'She likes you, golden girl. You have beautiful manners and more than that, a kind heart. Gentle and sensible, she called you, and tells me that you're a distinct improvement on my usual girls.'

'Thank her for me.' There was a distinct snap in the warm voice. He was taunting her, hurting her with deliberate jibes, a dark note threading the deep tones of his voice. Almost she was tempted to retaliate in kind, but that common sense his grandmother had noticed came to her aid and stopped her. When it came to warfare Burke was infinitely more experienced than she was, ruthless beneath the urbane worldliness. He lived in the world of big business, cut-throat, gladiatorial, where only the winner survived.

'I'll do that.' As he swung the car into the curb outside her house he commanded softly, 'Lunch with me tomorrow.'

Faine bit her lip, hesitated, then, with a humiliating sense of her own lack of will-power when faced by his dominant masculinity, agreed.

At the door he kissed her, hard, holding her head still while his mouth made the kind of uncompromising demand she feared. Shocked, she put out her hand in rejection, but when it came into contact with the soft silk of his shirt her fingers spread and she stood, while his heart pounded into her palm and he took her mouth as though he starved for her.

When he lifted his head she groaned out his name.

'No,' he said beneath his breath, his hand cruel as he disentangled her fingers from his shirt. 'If I come in with you I'll take you to bed.'

'I don't care.'

He lifted her hand to his mouth and bit the fleshy mound beneath her thumb, hard enough to hurt, softly enough to make desire kick her in the loins.

'I do. Goodnight.'

It was no use protesting; she knew that implacable note in his voice. And she was tired enough to sleep almost instantly, though when she woke the next morning the bedclothes were in the kind of tangle which denoted a restless night.

Headachy, angry with herself for caving in so shamefully, she spent the morning mowing the lawn, giving herself just time to shower and wash her hair before the bell announced Burke's arrival.

He smiled at her, those shrewd eyes scrutinising her as if she was a new, unknown species of animal. She hated that cool examination; it stripped her of camouflage. It was as though each time he saw her he needed to probe beneath the surface as if she was an enemy whose weaknesses were important.

'You're always on time,' he said by way of greeting, and drew her towards him and kissed her forehead.

Faine brushed her lips across his cheek and said lightly, 'My parents brought me up to be punctual too. Where are we going?'

'Wait and see.'

'Am I dressed suitably?'

It was a stupid question, for it gave him the opportunity to survey the length of her body on the pretext of examining her clothes. That he enjoyed what he saw was clear; she disliked being made to feel like a slave chosen for her most basic requirements.

'Very suitably,' he said, a note of irony sharpening his voice. 'Let's go.'

He seemed almost on edge, his accent clipped, driving with a little less than his usual skill. Faine sat quietly, afraid as she had never been before, for this was a Burke she did not know, and she thought she knew what was going to happen next.

But her eyes widened as she realised where they were going and when the car drew up in front of the high, thick tangle of hedge right next door to the St Paul's Reserve she turned to stare at him, her expression asking the question she could not put into words.

He smiled. 'Let's go in.'

It was just the same, a secret, quiet place, loud with bee-song. In the wreckage of the old garden flowers had appeared, tall pink watsonias, little clumps of pinks, even a few thin, straggly seedling stocks. The flowers had reverted right back to single mauve blossoms but still gave forth that beautiful perfume. A chaffinch called loudly and monotonously, 'chink, chink, chink,' before singing a song composed of trills and flourishes.

The house dreamed quietly in its enchanted setting, Sleeping Beauty needing the kiss of the prince to wake it from slumber.

Faine stared around her, sighing, wishing—oh, wishing many things!

Then Burke took a key from his pocket and unlocked the door and she asked foolishly, 'Where on earth did you get that?'

'From the real estate agent who's been trying to sell the place for the past two years.' He grinned down at her and said with mocking emphasis, 'Darling, stop looking so taken aback! Would you like it?'

'*Like* it!' She stared up at him, totally bewildered. 'But what——'

'There's one condition,' he interrupted as if she hadn't spoken. 'I go with the house.' And then, after a long, frozen silence, 'I'm asking you to marry me, idiot. Stop looking so appalled, or you'll give me a complex! I've never asked anyone to marry me before; if you hurt my feelings now I might never pluck up the courage again.'

He meant her to smile, and she did, while disjointed thoughts whirled around her head, preventing her from saying anything to the point.

After a long moment she suddenly flushed, her heart beginning to beat again, and felt an overpowering surge of love. And knew, with an instinct older than time, that she could not express it. Whatever he wanted of her it was not a fervid outpouring of her emotions.

Unconsciously her teeth closed on her lower lip. She looked away, veiling with her lashes the leaping lights deep in her eyes.

'Faine?' He sounded surprised, a little aloof.

Immediately her glance flew back to the hard handsome face, locked there with his and in spite of every instinct she possessed she said slowly, 'Yes, of course I'll marry you.'

'You had me wondering for a moment.'

But as he pulled her into his arms she knew that he had expected nothing but her enthusiastic agreement. Then he kissed her, taking his time about it, and under the golden tide of desire his touch aroused in her the doubts and fears vanished for a time.

CHAPTER SIX

'WHEN?' Burke asked thickly against her mouth.

'Whenever you want.'

'How long a notice will you have to give?'

Faine lifted her head, staring into his eyes. 'A month. Don't you want me to keep on working?'

'No.' And he kissed her again, deliberately using his expertise to silence her. Through a haze of need and hunger she heard him say, 'Being my wife is going to be a full-time job, Faine. Will you mind living here while the place is renovated? We can rent a place if you'd hate it. I've had an architect look at it; he says that it's in remarkably good shape and unless you want to cut holes in walls it needs major alterations only in the kitchen and bathrooms.'

She needed the excuse to move from his arms, to regain control of herself. 'Well, let's go in and see, shall we?'

He knew, of course; his smile was touched with a certain sardonic quality as he unlocked the door, very much in command of the situation. And while they walked through the house she was acutely aware that for the moment he was letting her set the pace—but that would only last as long as he wanted it to.

The discovery that the house still had its original furniture in it gave her something else to think of.

'Why is all this here?' she asked.

He looked indifferently around the long drawing-room, far too full of heavy Victorian stuff but with one or two good pieces hidden in the prevailing gloom.

'I believe that the last owner was a maiden lady of extreme age who left the place to a charity with the proviso that the furniture stay here. It's included in the price of the house. Choose anything you like and the rest can be auctioned on behalf of the charity. This Victorian stuff is coming back into fashion, I believe.'

Faine stopped, staring with delighted disbelief at a serpentine chest of drawers beneath a picture of a very haughty lady in a low-cut dress and ringlets.

'This—this must be Sheraton,' she said in awed tones, running her finger across the polished top over cross-banding and inlaid decoration in what was almost certainly satinwood. 'Thank heavens they've kept everything dusted and polished.'

'I paid them to,' Burke observed coolly.

Faine's uneasiness increased. There was no reason

for it, nothing she could put her finger on as the cause, yet by the time they were eating lunch out on the steps she knew that she could not go through with this ridiculous engagement and the sooner she told him the better!

So she turned towards him, ignoring the long legs outstretched beside her, the lean, powerful lines of his body, ignoring her own reactions to him. And found him looking at her with ironic comprehension.

'No,' he said with great determination: 'Cold feet or not, there's no escape for you now, Faine.'

'How did you know?' Her despair was a darkness in her voice. 'How on earth do you read me so clearly?'

'Kindred spirits, perhaps?' He laughed without humour and pulled her across the warm stone of the step to tuck her in beside him. 'You've got steadily more nervous since you agreed to marry me. All those swift, sideways glances, as though I've suddenly developed horns and hooves and turned into the Dark Lord of Hades himself.'

'Horns and hooves would make you a satyr, or Pan,' she returned crisply.

'So I've got my legends mixed.' He chuckled deeply and pulled her across his knees, tilting her chin so that he could see her face more clearly. 'I haven't had the advantage of an education like yours.'

She shook her head bemusedly. 'Don't try to fool me! You might have got your education where and when you could, but it's a quality one.' The sun caught in her curls as she turned her face into his chest, away from those hard, too-perceptive eyes. He saw too much. The brain behind his eyes was razor-sharp, quick and brilliant, coldly analysing all the data his five senses fed it.

And yet when she rested against him like that, beneath the pulsing excitement his nearness afforded her there was complete trust. He was a man to rely on, she thought wearily, totally competent, the protective male personified.

'Thank you.'

He moved slightly so that his back was against one of the fluted pillars which held up the verandah roof. One hand rested on her thigh, its warmth seeping through the thin denim of her skirt. The other found the curve of her waist, the fingers splayed; he was not holding her there, but she knew that an attempt to move away from him would end in failure.

'You must be incredibly strong,' she murmured, lost in a torment of delight. 'I'm no light weight.'

His breath stirred her hair. 'You're not heavy, either. Very slender, in spite of your height. Are you afraid that I'll want to sleep with you now that you've agreed to marry me?'

Unerringly he had tracked her withdrawal to its source. Shock held her still, shock and a kind of intoxication at the images his words evoked.

'Should I be?'

'Never answer a question with another question, my dear. It's a dead giveaway.' The hand at her waist moved upwards, slid between the buttons of her blouse and cupped her breast. 'No, don't stiffen—and don't try to pull away. You know you like me touching you—as much as I like the feel of you in my hands. But I won't do anything more than you want. I'm not a crass adolescent, unable to prevent my needs from running away with my common sense. Ever since the first time I kissed you you've resented the fact that I can arouse you. I don't know why, unless you had a painful experience with that man you planned to marry years ago.'

Faine looked up, startled and afraid, her expression wary. 'How—oh, of course, our gossiping mutual friend Philippa—Costain, isn't it now?'

'Yes, she was only too eager to tell me all about it.' He kissed her lips lightly, stopping any further attempt at speech on her part. 'I know that he wanted money more than he wanted you. If you allowed those iron-clad principles of yours to relax after the engagement I can understand why you felt raw and cheated when he broke it off. Phil Costain said that for your age you were somewhat sheltered. No doubt you were shattered at the time, but you should be over it by now.'

'I am,' she mumbled, wondering why she didn't tell him that she was still as virginal as when she had been a schoolgirl. Oh, she had wanted Dougal, but not enough to give in to his pleadings.

'Not quite, I think,' Burke said lightly. 'But I promise you, there'll be no lustful urgings towards the bedroom. We've all our lives in front of us to enjoy each other.' He must have felt her instinctive reaction to this almost matter-of-fact statement, for he chuckled soundlessly, his hand on her leg sliding beneath the skirt to stroke with sensuous gentleness the soft inner skin of her thigh. 'And I mean enjoy!' For a moment his hand closed fiercely on her flesh, then he released her pushing her off his knee with an abruptness she welcomed, for it gave her the chance to turn her face away.

It was too late, of course. He knew exactly how he affected her, had known right from the start, and surely now that they were engaged there was no longer any need for her to hide her emotions?

Much later that night, after he had had dinner with her at her flat and they had listened to music together and talked quietly about books and made plans for a wedding six weeks away, Faine realised that he had not told her that he loved her. And for some reason she wept a little as she lay waiting for sleep to come, sad, lonely tears such as she had not shed since Dougal's betrayal.

Things seemed much better the next morning, of course, even though the day was misty-wet and warm, ideal for green growing things but not at all good for humans.

Burke called for her early as she didn't go to the library until noon, and took her to a jeweller's where they chose, after some discussion, a ring with a magnificent canary-coloured diamond.

'Not the same colour as your eyes,' Burke told her with a twist of the lips which might have passed for a smile to someone who loved him less. 'I've never been very fond of orange topazes.'

Faine said nothing, staring down at the beautiful thing on her finger. The rings had had no price on them, but she would have had to be an idiot not to realise that they were in a price bracket far beyond anything she had ever dreamed of wearing. She had chosen from beautiful emeralds and rubies, an enormous sapphire of incredibly vivid blue—the fact that her ring was with them made her realise, as not even his opulent car had, just how wealthy Burke was.

She looked at him and he grinned down at her, pale eyes very shrewd. 'Having third thoughts? Too late, my darling. I told you before, there's no escape.'

The jeweller came fussily back, took Burke to one side and began talking softly. Faine heard the word 'insurance' and found herself swallowing very hard. The jewel on her finger glittered in the discreet, perfect light; it felt oddly light for such a big stone. Around it scintillated white diamonds in a setting which emphasised the exquisite colour of the gem. On her long slender hand it looked superb, a rich man's gift to the woman he had chosen for his wife.

After a few moments during which Burke spoke softly but with a cold incisiveness which gave her a glimpse of just how the money for her ring had been obtained, he turned and took her arm.

'Come on, I'll shout you morning tea and then take you back to work.'

'Don't you have to be anywhere?'

He shrugged. 'One of the advantages of being the boss is that I get to set the times. No, I left the morning free.'

'You were that sure of me?'

His fingers tightened on her arm. 'No. I hoped. What's worrying you, Faine? Afraid I might beat you? I think I can promise you that I'm house-trained.'

How could she say, *You haven't told me you love me. I'm afraid that you might be buying the best wife, just as you've bought the best car and the best ring.* How could she tell him that she was afraid that he could hurt her so badly that Dougal's betrayal would be nothing, a scratch compared to a lost limb?

She couldn't.

'It's a big step,' she said, trying to ignore the way women looked at him, that swift flash of awareness in almost every glance.

'You must have known it was coming.'

This time she shrugged, her smile very wry. 'No, how could I? You don't give much away. I knew you didn't want an affair—at least, it didn't seem as if you did. But marriage—well, that's a different ball game. Most men don't arrive at your age still single unless they've a good idea of how to keep themselves free from entanglements.'

There was a dry note in his voice as he replied, 'There have been entanglements, of course.'

'You know what I meant.'

'Yes.' They had reached a small coffee bar like hundreds of others, but one where Burke was clearly known. The waitress smiled adoringly at him before transferring her extremely interested glance to Faine as she wheeled the trolley up with its delicious burden of cakes.

'Just coffee,' Faine said quickly, her stomach rebelling at the thought of eating now.

'What will you have for lunch?'

She smiled. 'Yoghurt.'

'Then you'd better have something a little more solid now.'

One of her brows lifted as she looked at him. 'Being bossy, Burke?'

'You don't know me at all,' he returned, and put his hand over hers and squeezed it. 'You don't want me to worry about you, do you?'

She laughed, colour touching her cheeks, as a glint of mockery appeared in his steady regard.

'No, never. Tell me,' as she indicated a small slice of some fruit loaf, 'do you always get your own way?'

'Invariably.' His voice was bland, but there was a positive ring to it that made her look up sharply. 'You see,' he said with cool aplomb, 'I have very few scruples. It helps.'

'And that's a warning which should make me take to my heels in fear.'

'Ah, but you won't, will you?'

For a moment she toyed with the idea of striking back at his enormous self-assurance, but his glance on her was mocking and tolerant, and beneath it she blushed, for she wouldn't, and he knew why.

The coffee, superbly fragrant, saved her pride. The waitress arrived with a tall silver coffee pot, poured for them then wished them a very interested 'good morning' before attending to her other customers. The moment passed, but even after Burke had dropped her off after arranging to collect her from work that night she remembered his calm confidence. He knew that her physical attraction was so strong that it overcame her fears and doubts; he could see through the relaxed, sensible projection of her personality to the woman with fierce needs who made up the other half of Faine Hellier. Always she had tried to deny that woman with her primitive, earthy instincts, but he must have known right from the beginning that she existed. His perception made her feel naked and vulnerable, too open to hurt and pain. Especially as she had no such intuition. Oh, she knew what his persona projected. Astute, brilliant, civilised, worldly, with strong sexual magnetism—the adjectives came easily to mind. Too easily, because there were others which seemed just as appropriate, like ruthless, and cold, callous and dangerous.

That afternoon she did not wear her ring, nor did she tell Heather, but in the car Burke slipped it on her finger, saying, 'My grandmother will want to see it.'

'Will Gavin and Libby be there?'

'Yes.' He cursed under his breath as a car in front of them hared through a red light.

'It will be nice to see them again.' She stared out into the half darkness, strangely tired. 'It's been a while—in fact I've only met them two or three times.'

'They're looking forward to welcoming you into the family. My grandmother is ecstatic and will no doubt embarrass you immensely by referring to her desire for great-grandchildren as soon as possible.'

Deep inside her something jerked, a pain that was pleasurable. 'How about you?' she asked, trying to pretend that the subject didn't thrill and frighten her at the same time.

'I'm thirty-two. I'd rather not wait too long, but you, my girl, are the one who's going to have to carry my baby for nine months. The ultimate decision will be yours.'

'Then—not straight away.' Her fingers were weaving complicated patterns together in her lap, but her voice was commendably steady as she went on, 'I think I'd rather get used to being married before—before we have children.'

'Fair enough.' He dropped his hand over her writhing, restless ones until they stilled, then slanted a smile her way. 'Kind, sensible, jittery Faine! It will work. Try not to let those girlish qualms run away with you.' His mouth twisted. 'I'm sure I've read somewhere that the engagement period is supposed to be the happiest time of a woman's life. No pretty illusions stripped away by the sordid realities of living with a man.'

'That sounds like a hysterical Victorian,' she retorted smartly. 'Masculine, of course, who talked about "the little woman" and insisted the piano legs be covered in muslin so that her tender sensibilities wouldn't be shocked!'

'I knew that hair colour denoted a temper some-where,' Burke observed, and began to laugh as she turned towards him, her sparkling eyes enormous in the creamy oval of her face. 'No—no, don't fly at me! I'd rather we had our first fight over something of more importance! I know you're nervous—I'm not too sure whether I've done the right thing myself, if you must force me to be so ungallant, but I'm sure that's just the last futile resistance of a bachelor spirit. So stop trying to pick a fight with me, honey girl, and relax. I'm not a Prince Charming on a white charger, but let's face it, you're no Cinderella either.' His voice had hardened; now he sounded as if he was pointing out the advantages of some business merger. 'We click in all the right ways, Faine. You know that, it's why you agreed to marry me.'

Silence while she looked down at her hands, pale shapes in the dim interior of the car. 'Yes,' she agreed when it was clear that he was waiting for an answer. 'I'm sorry, I'm behaving badly. I suppose bachelor spirits can belong to both sexes. Mine seems to be making a fighting withdrawal.'

Which was a lie. She knew why she was edgy, and it had nothing to do with any desire for the freedom of spinsterhood. What she wanted was reassurance from him in the only way that mattered. Why wouldn't he say that he loved her?

The answer, of course, was pitifully obvious. Because he didn't. Sophisticated as he was, Burke probably didn't believe in the sort of love she craved. Plenty didn't nowadays. Perhaps he thought that their mutual desire and companionship were enough. Their tastes were basically similar, with just enough difference to be stimulating, and she had only to look at the lean

Yours **FREE** with a home subscription to
SUPER**ROMANCES**™

Now you never have to miss reading the newest **SUPERROMANCES**... because they'll be delivered right to your door.

Start with your free *Love beyond Desire*. You'll be enthralled by this powerful love story...from the moment Robin meets the dark, handsome Carlos and finds herself involved in the jealousies, bitterness and secret passions of the Lopez family. Where her own forbidden love threatens to shatter her life.

Your free *Love beyond Desire* is only the beginning. A subscription to **SUPERROMANCE** lets you look forward to a long love affair. Month after month, you'll receive four love stories of heroic dimension. Novels that will involve you in spellbinding intrigue, forbidden love and fiery passions.

You'll begin this series of sensuous, exciting contemporary novels...written by some of the top romance novelists of the day...with four every month.

And this big value...each novel, almost 400 pages of compelling reading...is yours for only $2.50 a book. Hours of entertainment every month for so little. Far less than a first-run movie or pay-TV. Newly published novels, with beautifully illustrated covers, filled with page after page of delicious escape into a world of romantic love...delivered right to your home.

A compelling love story of mystery and intrigue... conflicts and jealousies... and a forbidden love that threatens to shatter the lives of all involved with the aristocratic Lopez family.

Mail this card today for your FREE gifts.

TAKE THIS BOOK
AND TOTE BAG FREE!

Mail to: **SUPERROMANCE**
1440 South Priest Drive, Tempe, Arizona 85281

YES, please send me FREE and without any obligation, my **SUPERROMANCE** novel, *Love Beyond Desire*. If you do not hear from me after I have examined my FREE book, please send me the 4 new **SUPERROMANCE** books every month as soon as they come off the press, I understand that I will be billed only $2.50 per book (total $10.00). There are no shipping and handling or any other hidden charges. There is no minimum number of books that I have to purchase. In fact, I may cancel this arrangement at any time. *Love Beyond Desire* and the tote bag are mine to keep as FREE gifts even if I do not buy any additional books.

134-CIS-KADD

Name	(Please Print)	

Address		Apt. No.

City		

State		Zip

Signature   (If under 18, parent or guardian must sign.)

This offer is limited to one order per household and not valid to present subscribers. We reserve the right to exercise discretion in granting membership. If price changes are necessary you will be notified. Offer expires July 31, 1983.

PRINTED IN U.S.A.

EXTRA BONUS
MAIL YOUR ORDER
TODAY AND GET A
FREE TOTE BAG
FROM SUPERROMANCE.

Mail this card today for your FREE gifts.

elegance of his body to want to make love with him.

'O.K.?' he asked quietly.

She nodded, at last accepting that while it hurt to know that she was the one who loved, it would be far more painful to cut him from her life. He had the power to make the sun shine for her. And if a seductive little voice in her brain whispered that perhaps he might grow to return her feelings, she kept it to the back of her mind.

'Yes,' she said, stifling an unconscious sigh. 'No more stupidities, I promise you. I'll be sensible.'

The lights of a passing car showed his smile, appreciative as though he understood her only too well 'Not too sensible, I hope. I rather liked the glimpse I got of an angry golden girl, curls quivering, eyes glittering like hot topazes. Delectable—and extremely provocative.'

His voice was perfect for making love, smooth yet with an underlying depth of desire which excited her.

'Don't,' she said, mockery plain in her words, 'don't you *dare* say that I look beautiful when I'm angry!'

He laughed, turning the wheel into the drive of his home, and parked the car before saying, 'No, my darling, I won't. But it won't stop me from thinking it.'

They were all there, Libby and Mrs Guilford and Gavin. After the initial stiffness it should have been a pleasant evening but there were undercurrents which made Faine uneasy. Mostly, she decided, they came from Gavin. He sat in his wheelchair, thin face set in lines of recklessness which must have been habitual even before the accident. Now there was a defiant glitter in the deep blue eyes and he watched everyone, especially his wife and Burke, as though he resented with consuming anger the fact that they could walk.

He spoke to Libby with pseudo-pleasantness; it did not take long for Faine to detect the need to hurt beneath the orders phrased as requests, the quick comments which sounded innocuous until the bitter sting beneath registered. Libby was gentle and very wary. Her eyes seldom left him. She seemed to try to anticipate his every wish and need, hovering close to him, tense beneath the surface gaiety.

Almost as if he made her feel guilty, Faine thought, and wondered just how Gavin had been hurt. Once Libby laughed at something Burke said, but her glance immediately fled towards her husband and the moment's pleasure disappeared as she moved back to be closer to him. Gavin demanded another drink. While it was being poured he asked, 'And when is the happy occasion?'

'In about six weeks' time,' Burke replied evenly, his gaze cool and inflexible as it rested on his brother's features.

A faint colour touched Faine's cheeks as Gavin's malicious gaze came to rest at her waist. 'Any reason for the hurry?'

'Gavin!' Libby's cry had a note of pain to it and the liquid in the glass she was bringing to him slopped over the side.

'None but the usual one.' Burke's deep calm voice overrode his sister-in-law's protest. He fixed his eyes on his brother, continuing with a cool deliberation that brought dark colour to Gavin's skin, 'There's no need to wait. Faine has to work out a month's notice and after that she'll need a couple of weeks to organise things. We don't intend to have an enormous affair.'

'O.K., O.K., point taken.' Gavin grinned at Faine, but there was a kind of wicked misery in his expression which warned her that he hadn't finished. 'How do you feel about sharing the house with all of us? I think you're extremely brave to take us on.'

'Faine won't be,' Burke said calmly. 'I've bought a house on St Paul's Point.'

That was news to them all it was plain. Mrs Guilford asked exactly where—Faine had to rid herself of the idea that she was stepping into some breach—and in the ensuing conversation the effect of Gavin's remarks was glossed over. For the rest of the evening he said very little, but whenever Faine looked his way he was watching her from beneath his lashes. Each time their eyes met he gave her a mocking smile and each time it was she who looked away first.

On the way home Burke said tiredly. 'I'm sorry you had to cope with Gavin.'

'It's all right,' she told him, speaking too quickly.

'No, it's not. If he were any sort of a man he would have found some way of coming to terms with the situation. Instead, he sits and broods and does his level best to make the life of everyone who loves him a living hell. He's had time enough. The hospital psychiatrist said that he should be past the worst. He always had a malicious streak; it seems that he's going to give in to it.'

Faine sighed, thinking of the thin figure in that wheelchair, his lounging pose belied by the tension of his body. 'He looks—he looks as though he knows something that horrifies and excites him at the same time. How was he hurt?'

'Racing.'

'So Libby had nothing to do with it?'

The car leapt forward under the influence of a foot carelessly heavy. 'No,' he said, his voice expressionless. 'Not a thing. Why?'

Somehow she had said something she shouldn't. Carefully, keeping her tone neutral, she replied, 'It's just that she seems to feel guilty. She laughed only once during the evening and almost immediately she stopped and went back to him, as though she was being disloyal.'

They had come to a part of the road notorious for its accidents. After it had been negotiated Burke said positively 'Libby has nothing to feel guilty about. She does, of course, but it's only the natural guilt all those unaffected feel in the presence of the handicapped. I honestly think that if she could she'd change places with him.' A pause, and then he said aloofly, 'And Gavin, being what he is, would accept such a sacrifice.'

The cool contempt in his tones chilled her. 'You're hard on him.'

'I know my brother. Although I'm fond of him I can't shut my eyes to his failings. He's busy making miserable as many lives as he can. He'll try it with you, too. I noticed him this evening, watching you, doing his best to make you uneasy.'

'Succeeding, too,' Faine admitted.

He nodded. 'Ignore it. After we're married we won't see much of them. I'm not having you upset by his spitefulness.'

And there the matter rested.

CHAPTER SEVEN

THEY were married late on a summer's day in the small church Faine attended just around the corner from her flat. She had chosen to wear silk chiffon, the colour jersey cream, the frilled jacket, long gathered skirt and narrow camisole top sprinkled with small gold beads, while around her narrow waist she wore a twisted gold belt of silk cord. Her only jewellery were her mother's Victorian pearl earrings and her engagement ring. She carried orchids, cream and gold with cool green throats, and wore high gold Italian sandals. The whole outfit had cost a breathtaking amount of money, but she was determined not to be overshadowed by any of the guests. She had no attendants, but Anna and Heather fussed enough for ten bridesmaids and Stu gave her away, terrified that he would do something call down Anna's wrath on his head.

A Hellier cousin and her husband came up from Hawkes Bay, but apart from that the other guests were friends. Mrs Guilford had insisted on the reception being held at the St Heliers house. Faine had no idea where the wedding night was to be spent. She had not asked. These past weeks Burke had become more and more distant, as if his misgivings about marriage had solidified into definite objections.

A week before the wedding Faine observed quietly, after an evening spent listening to music, 'There's still time to call it off.'

He turned his head to look at her, very composed. 'Why?'

Shrugging, gauche beneath that ironic gaze, she said, 'You don't seem exactly interested.'

Amused understanding gleamed in his expression. 'No?' He extended a hand and cupped the nape of her neck, pushing his fingers into the soft curls.

Faine bit her lip and jerked away, or tried to, for as soon as she moved his fingers twisted cruelly and he pulled her half across him, her head bent forward so that he could reach her neck and shoulder with his mouth. Before she had met him she had never realised how sensitive certain areas of her body were; now she trembled as he kissed the nape of her neck, an arm across her breasts holding her still as his other hand smoothed her hair away to leave a clear path for his mouth. At first the kisses were gentle, but soon she began to feel the pressure of his teeth against her skin. Against her shoulder blades his heart beat and thundered, as though her subservient attitude excited him.

'Burke!' she exclaimed, trying to straighten up.

He laughed beneath his breath and turned her so that she was lying across his knees, her face open to his gaze. She looked up at the hard, exciting lines and planes of his, the magnificent bone structure beneath tanned skin, the cool blaze in his pale eyes, the twisted smile as he captured her mouth beneath his in a kiss that annihilated time and space.

When it ended she was lying half beneath him, pinned to the sofa by his body as he slid his arms beneath her shoulders, lifting her to expose her throat to his hungry kisses. Faine's hands slid beneath his shirt to caress and cling, her skin heated with a passion that left her breathing in jerky gasps, her whole being centred on the merciless contractions his hands and mouth and the weight of his body were arousing deep within her.

For the first time ever she knew what it was to be racked by lust, burned by an importunate need to take and be taken. From beneath his lashes Burke's eyes glittered fiercely. Shivering, aching with desire, Faine tried to push him away, for something cruel and coldly impersonal in his passion frightened her.

Instantly his arm slid further down her back until its movement lifted her hips free of the cushions. And then he forced her mouth open and moved to lower himself on to her, using a technique refined by hundreds of such encounters in the past to make her whimper with pain and frustration. He was heavy, but she would gladly have put up with the discomfort of her position if only he would satisfy the needs he had aroused so quickly and so brutally.

Horrified, she realised that she was pleading with him, begging him to release her from the dark shell of her own sensuality, her voice saying over and over again, 'Please . . . oh, please . . .'

As if her violent response had taken him by surprise he drew a deep breath, then lay still, his mouth warm against her throat until his heartbeats slowed. Then he lifted himself away from her, pulling her up with him until they were once more upright.

'No,' he said quietly, holding her chin when she would have hidden her shamed face. 'No, when I take you for the first time it's going to be properly, with the whole night to enjoy you.' He smiled and lifted her hand to his mouth, kissing the tips of her fingers. 'You respond with such gratifying enthusiasm, my darling, that a hurried encounter here wouldn't be making the most of your charms.'

'I think your self-control frightens me,' she muttered, unable to free herself from her impression of deliberate, calculated passion.

He shrugged, his glance quick and sharp. 'I hope I've convinced you that it isn't lack of interest,' he replied with a return to his usual aloofness, adding with a slight smile, 'Your brand of provocation is potent enough to make even a saint lose command of himself!'

'But not you?'

'Ah, but I'm no saint.'

Alone at last after her charming little wedding, Faine found herself shivering as she changed from her beautiful dress to one in her favourite soft blouson style.

For months, it seemed, she had ached for Burke, some of her dreams had been troubled by his enigmatic figure while others had been amazingly erotic!

Now, before too many hours were past, she would be his wife in every sense of the word. The thought made her cheeks hot; she pressed her hands to them and stood quietly, breathing deeply and carefully. Then, firmly keeping her mind on what she was doing, she smoothed down her dress of silk crêpe-de-chine, pulled the jacket in matching blue over her shoulders and picked up her bag.

Outside the sun had gone down in a blaze of soft tangerine and rose red. Now the sky in the west was green, deepening to indigo overhead. Only Venus was bright enough to show against the brilliance, a great, coolly shining star in the west. In the magnolia tree outside the window a blackbird sang its piercingly sweet evensong. Through the foliage Faine could see the lights beyond the houses, the vast spread of glitter which was Auckland. Perfume drifted along the quiet air, spicy-sweet. With her eyes she followed it to its source, an Australian frangipani tree, its flowers like cream and gold stars against the glossy green leaves.

Nervous tension made her restless; she leaned out and saw Burke beneath the pergola, standing tall under a cloud of white and blue clematis. He had given her his room and was changing in a guest bedroom on the ground floor. Presumably he was ready.

Faine sped softly out of the room and down the stairs, mercifully meeting no one as she made her way to the room where he'd changed. Inside it was dark. She stood a moment, getting her bearings, and was just about to move across to the French windows when someone out of sight spoke from behind him in the depths of the pergola.

It was Libby, her voice barely above a whisper. 'Be happy,' she said, and in the two simple words there was all the confirmation of Faine's unspoken, inchoate suspicions.

But there was more. Faine stood, unbreathing, as Burke jerked around, saying in a wrenched voice, 'Oh, *God*! I can't——'

'Yes, yes, you can—you must.' They were standing apart, facing each other like antagonists, but now Libby stretched out her hand and laid it against his cheek. 'She—she's a dear, I like her so much, and she'll make you happy. She's so practical and sensible that—that——'

'That she won't miss—*this*!' In the deeper darkness beneath the pergola the two shadows merged into one in an embrace that made Faine draw a breath as sharp as a sword to the heart.

They did not hear her. They would have heard nothing, so lost in each other they were. She could not move, could not force herself away from this cruel death of all her hopes. The most reluctant voyeur in all the world, she stayed motionless, watching as Burke kissed his sister-in-law with a starving passion too long repressed.

'Darling,' Libby whispered, 'oh, darling, darling, *darling* . . . You must go. Please . . . Burke, it's getting late. She'll be ready.'

Faine winced, waiting for him to consign his new wife to hell, but he said heavily, 'Yes, I must go. My heart's delight, I'm glad you came to me—finally.'

'I couldn't bear not to say goodbye.' The smooth dark head lifted. Libby was speaking into his throat, each word heavy with despair and desire. 'I didn't want this to happen—all these months and there's been nothing to reproach myself for.' Her voice altered, became fierce. 'But I'm *glad*! *Glad!* At least I'll have this to remember.'

'Darling . . .' They kissed once more, her arms locked behind his head, his across her back and hips, so close that Faine felt nausea clog her throat. She knew what they were feeling, the rising desire, the excitement kindling passion as their mouths fused together.

Then, so abruptly that Libby staggered, Burke put her from him. 'Goodbye, my dearest,' he said, and watched as she walked away before turning and making his way into the house.

Straight past Faine. Even then he might not have known she was there except that he switched the light on.

Shock turned him white. He stood, with his finger on the light switch, staring at her as if he literally could

not believe the evidence of his eyes. Faine stared back,
too stupefied by what she had witnessed to be able to
hide her emotions. Her heart beat heavily in her throat,
almost in time with the muscle which jerked by his
mouth.

'How long have you been there?'

She shivered. 'Since just before she came.'

The shock had receded somewhat. Colour was
coming back into his skin and his eyes were once more
watchful, probing for an advantage.

'I see.' He dropped his hand and pulled his tie loose.
'I'm sorry,' he said, speaking gently. 'You've had a
hell of a shock. Can I get you something to drink?'

Her smile was a masterpiece of irony. 'No, thank
you. I've had quite enough.'

'Two glasses of champagne?' He tugged at a cufflink,
frowned and said impatiently, 'Here, take these
damned things out, will you? Gran insisted I wear her
husband's ones and they're practically impossible to
get rid of single-handed.'

So her first—and last—task as his wife was to remove
his cufflinks. They were big, old-fashioned things,
diamonds set in gold, not what you'd expect to see on
a man as contemporary as Burke, but he wore them
with such panache that they became suitable accessories.

As her fingers worked them free he slipped his arm
around her shoulders, saying quietly, 'We'll work it
out, Faine.'

And suddenly she was very angry. 'Work what out?'
she asked, moving away to drop the links on a chest of
drawers. 'Shouldn't you be saying that to Libby?
There's nothing for us to *work out*.'

Burke pulled his shirt off and dropped it, his expression remote and cold. 'What do you mean by that?'

'Well, obviously there's no chance of our marriage succeeding.'

'Why?'

She stared at him, unaware of the fact that he was still stripping off. '*Why?* For the most obvious reason! When I agreed to marry you I didn't realise that there was another woman in possession.'

He was fully in command of himself once more, hauling a dark shirt over broad shoulders. 'She is not, never has been, in possession.'

'You know what I mean.'

'Yes.' He flung his trousers on the bed, took a pair from a hanger in the wardrobe and pulled them on, then said calmly, 'I know exactly what you mean. Why the sudden revulsion? I don't remember you asking at any time whether I was in love with anyone else. And as I have very carefuly avoided telling you that I love you, you could have had no illusions.'

Faine turned away, sick and helpless, her hands clasped tightly together while she fought a desolation of spirit so intense she thought she would never recover from it.

'Could you?' he probed, coming up behind her to take her by the shoulders. 'Did you think that, Faine?'

Momentarily she closed her eyes. 'No, I didn't,' she told him savagely, her pride and her anger reviving her. 'But have you any idea just how degrading it is to be used as a substitute? I won't allow you to—to pretend when you . . .' Her voice faded as he turned her. She held herself stiffly, aware that she was too overwrought to be able to think clearly while he who should by rights have been equally upset, having just renounced the love of his life, was fully in control of both himself and the situation.

'When I make love to you?' Burke finished softly. 'You're surprisingly unsophisticated in some ways; I keep forgetting that fact. Believe me, when I make love to you, Faine, you'll be no substitute. I'm sorry that you overheard—what you did—but it need make very little difference to us.'

'I can't believe I'm hearing this!' She put her hands over her ears, fighting hard for control. 'I'm sorry, but I can't go through with it. You lied—oh, not directly, but you know you lied! Can't you see that it makes all of the difference in the world? If I'd thought for one moment that you and Libby——'

'There was *nothing*! All that's between us you saw just now. And there will never be anything. My wedding vows are important to me. I intend keeping them.'

He would too. No matter who got hurt in the process.

'Well, I don't intend keeping mine,' she returned harshly, 'In fact——'

His hands on her shoulders tightened, biting deep into her flesh. Faine stopped speaking, her features twisting in pain at this unexpected brutality.

'You'll do what I want,' he said between his teeth, anger lighting cold fires in the depths of his eyes. He looked as though he could kill her. 'I'm not going to have all my plans set aside because of some last-minute virginal qualms. Are you ready?'

'Yes, but——'

'But nothing.' He released her, stepped back to ask with cold deliberation, 'Tell me, how had you planned to tell my grandmother that you'd changed your mind?'

Beneath the piercing probe of his glance she paled. With unerring aim he had hit her exactly where she was most vulnerable. During the weeks of their engagement she had grown very fond of Ellen, coming to appreciate just how much this marriage and the prospect of great-grandchildren meant to the older woman.

'Damn you,' she whispered. 'Damn you, Burke!'

For answer he smiled with cruel determination and took her by the elbow, turning her towards the door.

Ever after Faine could remember little of the farewells; the only thing that impinged was the warmth of Ellen Guilford's kiss on her cheek. And the moment when topaz eyes met deep blue at the door and for a moment Libby could not hide her stark anguish. Or a bitter jealousy.

Shaken, cold with reaction, Faine allowed herself to be put into the same silver-grey monster she had seen at that first meeting, and even turned to wave goodbye. The shock of betrayal had robbed her of energy and will-power, damping down her reactions. She felt inordinately tired and yawned twice, covering her mouth with a hand that felt boneless and limp.

Burke's head turned as he looked at her, but when she made no effort to acknowledge him he switched his attention back to the road, driving with his usual skill through the thin traffic towards the north. Faine leaned her head against the headrest, staring into the darkness with eyes that saw nothing as the car swept on.

Incredibly she must have slept, for it was the sudden quiet as the engine stopped that woke her, heavy-eyed and cross, to the realisation that they had reached their destination.

It was very still, so dark that she knew they were a
long way from a road, but from somewhere in front of
them a wide sheet of water glimmered palely in the
light of the stars. Not the sea, she deduced, for there
was no sound of waves.

'I'll take our bags in and put the lights on.' Burke's
voice was cool and dispassionate.

He didn't wait for an answer but swung out of his
seat, leaving Faine to unclip her safety-belt. Once out
of the car she felt better, drawing in deep breaths of
the air, tangy with the unmistakable tinge of salt, that
scent that speaks of long beaches salt-bloomed, of red
cliffs, of the myriads of inhabitants in the secret little
world of the rock pools, of death and life and the sensuous delights of water and sand and sun against the
skin.

About twenty yards away lights bloomed in a building, destroying in an instant her communion with the
night. Every nerve in her body tensed; the hand against
her thigh clenched, and was slowly relaxed.

'Faine?' She could not answer, and Burke said her
name again in a sharp voice.

'By the car.'

'I can see you now.' He appeared beside her, an incredibly silent mover for such a big man and touched
her arm. 'Come inside.'

It had to be now. Once she allowed him to take her
inside it would be tantamount to agreeing to sleep with
him. In a voice ragged with tension she said, 'I'm not
going to go through with this, Burke. I can't.'

'All right.' He smiled as her head jerked towards
him and touched her cheek. 'I'm not an insensitive
yokel, my dear. You've had a hell of a shock and it
would be an act of monumental stupidity to force you

into something you're not ready for. I don't want you hating me. I'll ask no more from you than you want to give.' His hand lifted, he pulled her towards him and held her a moment in a gesture of comfort. 'The first thing a businessman learns,' he said, his voice revealing that he smiled as he spoke, 'is when to apply pressure and when to be patient. An impatient speculator goes down the drain very rapidly.'

'I suppose that's meant to be reassuring!'

He bent his head to listen to her muffled tones and replied on a note of laughter, 'I could reassure you much more effectively.'

Bitterness rose like a choking gag in her throat. How could he be so—so *lighthearted* about this situation? She didn't know him at all. Later it occurred to her that perhaps he was trying to make things easier for both of them on this most peculiar of wedding nights. Only twenty-four hours ago she had lain in her bed telling herself with heaven knew how many thrills that that would be the last time she slept alone. She had drifted off to sleep and into a dream so erotic that even now she blushed at the remembrance of it.

And presumably Burke too had thought of tonight with some anticipation. Men could make love without feeling anything more than desire. Or perhaps he had whipped up desire by pretending that she was Libby.

The night air was suddenly cold on her skin. Shivering, she stepped away from him, saying with a frigid lack of expression, 'I doubt if anything you could do would reassure me.'

A short silence before he observed coolly, 'Any other man might take that for a challenge.'

'I'm *so* glad you're not any other man,' she returned, sarcasm a sharp thread in her voice.

'Well, that's a start, at least.' As if her rebuff hadn't registered he took her by the shoulder and turned her towards the house. 'Let's go in. You're cold and I'm tired. Mind the path—it's crushed shell and occasionally a pebble will catch a high heel and tip it.'

Inside the house was big and cool, polished wood floors, painted walls in sea colours, furniture with spare lines, sleek and modern in wood and stainless steel. Books on white-painted shelves against a wall provided the only decoration.

'You don't like it,' said Burke as she stood looking around her.

'I do. It's—different.'

'You can alter what you like.' He gestured towards a door on the other side of the room. 'Bedrooms through there. Yours is the second door on the right.'

Every instinct warned her that she was courting danger, but she had to ask. 'Where are you sleeping?'

Mockery gleamed in the depths of his eyes. 'Across the hall. I'm going to make the bed up now.'

'Shall I?'

His lips moved without the slightest humour, his expression set in a hard, taunting smile. 'No, my dear, you will not. Not unless you intend me to forget every good resolution I've been making for the past hour and take you without form or ceremony.'

A wave of colour rushed through her skin; she looked away, cursing herself for her idiocy.

'No, I thought not,' he said with ironic emphasis. 'Why don't you unpack? I'll make us a drink and then we can get to bed. If I'd known that getting married was so exhausting I could well have changed my mind.'

A pity you didn't, Faine thought wearily. Then

neither of them would be trapped in this mockery of a marriage. If only she knew *why* he had done it, why he had deliberately courted her, wooed her into marriage in spite of his feeling for Libby. Always, always behind his passion there had been that great depth of reserve; from the first Faine had sensed it, but, naïve fool that she was, she had ignored her intuition, hoping that her growing love would summon a like response from him.

No doubt he thought that she wanted the same things from a marriage as he so clearly did—passion, companionship, a family. But he must have known that such a marriage was doomed to failure, loving Libby as he did.

Unless ... her hands stilled amongst her clothes. Unless he hoped that marriage would take his mind off his impossible love, as well as provide him with an heir and an amenable wife to be his hostess. Very carefully, as if the future course of her life depended on it, she folded a cotton knit shirt and put it away into a drawer. It was so quiet that she could hear the soft noise made by little inch-high waves as they creamed up on to the beach somewhere below the house. Somewhere, high above, a plane droned across the sky, already descending, on its way to the airport at Mangere. From Hawaii, she thought, or perhaps Rarotonga, magic names of Polynesia.

Burke hadn't asked her where she wanted to go for this honeymoon. Just told her that as he had only a week to spare they'd be unable to go any distance. And she had smiled, and told him to surprise her.

Hot tears stung her eyes. He had done that, and more.

A hand pressed to her mouth, she blinked furiously. Now was not the time to weep, to rail aloud at the gods for their unfairness. More than anything else she needed to retain command of herself, hiding the fact that her self-respect was in shreds. The man she had fallen in love with did not exist; that had to be faced and dealt with, but not tonight, not when she was so tired, so emotionally fragile.

Normally she was courageous. Her years alone had strengthened an already strong character and she could cope with anything, even the shattering of all her hopes. But she needed time, and she was very much afraid that time was exactly what she wasn't to be granted. Burke had accepted the inevitable, but beneath the cool sophisticated surface there was a man of buccaneering instincts. You did not, she thought wearily, transform a stake of thousands into an empire worth millions in ten years without having implacable determination and a strong streak of gambler's recklessness. Well hidden it might be, but it was there; this marriage was just another indication of it. How long Burke would be content to wait without forcing the issue depended entirely on his character, and she had just forced herself to accept the fact that she knew nothing of him.

The sound of her name and his fingers tapping on the door made her jump guiltily as if she had been planning an escape.

'I'm coming!' she called, hastily thrusting the rest of her clothes into a drawer.

He had made her hot milk and poured into it a generous tot of brandy—not her favourite drink, but she sipped slowly, realising that it would help her sleep, and followed his lead in conversation, talking quietly about the events of the day, filling any silence which threatened to be awkward with the kind of easy social coin she knew so well how to dispense. Probably another reason why he had chosen her to marry, she thought aridly, conscious of his watchful regard and the heat across her cheeks and throat.

'You're hot,' he remarked.

As she shook her head the light from a lamp caught in gold threads through her curls. 'Brandy always gives me a hectic flush. Burke, how far has the house been finished?'

Although she did not then realise it, it was capitulation, and he looked keenly at her before the broad shoulders moved in the smallest of shrugs. 'The structural alterations are finished. At the moment they're completing the kitchen and the bathrooms. There was surprisingly little to do, you know. It's always been well cared for; apart from the kitchen and bathrooms, all it needed was tidying up. My architect was thrilled to find such a perfect Georgian house.' He smiled rather sardonically. 'I had to insist that we wanted a modern kitchen and up-to-date plumbing. He muttered things about crass *nouveau riche* and photographed everything in sight before allowing one carpenter to touch the place.'

Faine stared, indignant, and Burke laughed softly. 'He's a very old friend. We've worked together often before. When you're angry your eyes are dark amber with glints of fire in the heart of them.'

The compliment was delivered in such a lazy drawl that the tinge of insolence to the words escaped her for a moment. When it registered she blushed and set the mug down, angry with him and with herself for being affected by his cheap flattery.

'I think it's time I went to bed,' she said, but yawned, thus effectively destroying the dignity of her tone.

The room spun very gently for a moment or so, then
steadied. She had eaten little all day and the brandy,
on top of the champagne at the reception, had gone
straight to her head. She blinked several times before
realising that Burke was in front of her, one lean strong
hand extended.

'No, I can manage,' she said, but ignoring her, he
grasped her wrist and jerked her up and into his arms,
holding her with hard purpose when she flinched away
and would have struggled.

'No,' he said, the deep voice suddenly harsh. 'Don't
treat me as if I've suddenly got leprosy. Last night you
kissed me and it wouldn't have taken any effort for me
to get you into bed. I'm still the same man.'

'I don't *believe* this!' she whispered despairingly. 'If
you can't see that things have changed——'

'Of course I can see it!' His fingers tightened on her
shoulders, bruising the fine skin. 'I know! If I didn't
I'd be making love to you now, and believe me, it
wouldn't be rape. Beneath all that injured innocence
you still want me, and the day is going to come when
you accept that. Then we can start to make something
of this marriage.'

'I *can't*!' she wailed, exhausted, stimulated by his
closeness, the rock-hard strength of him, the faint
erotic scent that taunted her senses. 'Oh, damn you,
Burke, I'm going to b-bawl and I haven't cried for
years. Let me g-go!'

'Crying doesn't go with the image, does it?' he
returned beneath his breath, giving her a little shake.
'Cry if you want to, but you're not going until I've
made you understand.'

'Oh, I understand all right.' Sheer rage dried her
tears, brought a sparkle to the depths of her gaze as

she lifted it to hold his. 'Only too well, in fact. You're in love with your sister-in-law. Some quixotic loyalty makes it impossible for you to go to bed with her, so you fixed on someone else, someone who was too thick to see beyond the end of her own nose, and married her instead—thereby satisfying in one blow your own dynastic instinct and your grandmother's hopes for descendants, your libido and your need for a hostess. Only you've failed, because I *will not* be treated as a stand-in for someone else! You may be basking in a conscious glow of rectitude because you haven't seduced your crippled brother's wife, but as far as I'm concerned you've betrayed whatever it is you feel for her, as well as me!'

She knew that her searing words would anger him, but she had not expected the ugly expression with which he dragged her close and kissed her with precise brutality, totally without tenderness, his mouth forcing hers open in an implacable invasion that was cruelly sensual. Faine choked, gasping for breath, and Burke lifted his head and said with icy command, 'That's exactly how I'll stop your mouth if you ever again speak to me like that!' His hands relaxed, slid down her shoulders to cover her breasts, each slow movement explicitly sexual, the hard pitiless glance daring her to protest and risk another vicious assault like the last.

Faine trembled, for the first time in her life afraid of a man in a situation she couldn't control. Her lips felt swollen and bruised, her whole being shrieked with outrage at his cold impersonal touch, but although she could hardly bear his hands on her she could not summon up the courage to move. It would take very little for them both to lose control, he driven by anger, she by this sense of betrayal; they stood facing each other like mortal enemies, bodies rigid, every instinct urging them on to battle.

But there could be only one end to such a battle, and she could not bear to have him take her in anger and contempt. Apart from the rape of her person she was afraid that he would be correct and that she would surrender to his overwhelming masculinity and the promptings of her love, and make him a gift of herself.

And if once that happened, if he knew that she loved him with all her soul, then she would be doomed.

So she stood, shaking, her features sharp and white, while his hands moved across her breasts in a slow, sensual tracing of every curve and contour, until finally he drew a deep breath, saying savagely, 'Oh, *God!* Don't look like that—Faine, are you *afraid* of me?'

When she looked up she surprised a flash of something perilously close to pain in his eyes before she looked away again.

He caught her chin and held it so that her face was open to him, and what he saw made him swear, crudely and pointedly, until she flushed and held back the words with the back of her hand.

Then his mouth moved into a kiss. As she jerked her hand away he said quietly, tiredly, 'I'm sorry, Faine. Don't be frightened of me. I have a vicious temper, but I very rarely lose control. I wouldn't do anything to hurt you. Please believe me.'

But you have, she wanted to scream, clenching her hands into fists because he was so insensitive that he didn't understand what he had done to her. You've almost killed me, and you don't even know it!

Perhaps something of her rage and torment showed in her expression, because he caught her hands and held them gently between his own. 'God, I'm sorry! I'm sorry that you heard the way you did and I know what you're feeling now.' His smile was fleeting, not at all humorous. 'The joke is on me. It was your pride that attracted me in the first place. You looked at me with such cool interest——'

Faine could have sworn that she made no movement. She could not, literally could not breathe for a moment, the pain was so intense. But he knew.

'I'm making things worse,' he said with self-contempt heavy in his voice. 'We're both too tired to think straight. But remember this, Faine. Hurt pride is a cold bedfellow—an old cliché, but like them all, true. Go to bed now. Things won't seem so bad in the morning.'

That night she dreamed again of masks and mirrors, but this time she knew what they meant.

CHAPTER EIGHT

SHE awoke before dawn and lay in the enormous double bed looking out through the window at a world which changed gradually from dark to pale grey, and then to full colour as the sun climbed up over the horizon. The room opened out on to two terraces through wide sliding glass doors. She discovered now that the side terrace faced east into a scrub-covered hillside, so that when she padded across the floor and pulled the curtains back it was to see the sun come over the rim of the hill, outlining the ragged skyline of manuka tips in gold for a second, before it resumed its joyous climb towards the zenith.

Not too far away sheep called, their shrill voices pleasantly muted on the cool clear air. On the bushes and the fence glinted traceries of spider webs outlined in crystal, perfect, delicate yet stronger than steel, patterned like lace against the darkness of the foliage. There was no wind, not even the hint of a breeze, yet through the window came the subtle scent of the sea and the spicy fragrance of the manuka scrub, scattered now with flowers as white as any star. It was the leaves that gave off that perfume, not the flowers, and the memory of it had the power to cause bitter homesickness in New Zealanders abroad.

Faine had slept well, heavily, with no tossing and turning. Now she lay quietly against the pillows, head aching slightly, eyes overbright, and tried hard to regain some peace of mind. At least, she thought wryly, at least Burke didn't know that she loved him. A bitter smile touched her lips. Would he have married her if he had known it? Somehow she doubted it.

Set some distance by the night from her discovery of yesterday, she was able to view it with a certain objectivity, which was as yet only surface deep. She must strive to make detachment an essential part of herself, for if she gave way to that bitter sense of betrayal which had precipitated her outburst last night she would drive herself into a breakdown. Thinking back, she realised that the only reason Burke had married her was because he believed that she didn't love him.

He had made that quite clear by his reference to her hurt pride. Unless, she thought wearily, he was offering a salve for that very pride. But a moment's thought convinced her otherwise. She had never revealed her love, never spoken it or given him cause to believe that she felt anything more for him than desire and that swift mental affinity which made them enjoy each other's company so much. Clearly he thought she had chosen him for those very reasons, as well as his money. She smiled with a hard lack of amusement at just how Burke would react if he ever discovered that she would have married him if he hadn't had a cent to his name.

A shag flew across to perch on a dry stump up the hill. Strange that so clumsy a flier should dive and swim so skilfully. She got out of bed again to pull back the curtains that led out on to the big terrace at the front of the house.

She was not surprised to see Burke swimming in the bay below. He must have moved extremely quietly to get outside without her hearing him. Like a tiger, she thought, and shivered, watching as he struck out for a reef beneath the low cliff at the western boundary of the bay. Wet, the copper hair was dark and sleek like a seal's. He was lucky that in this area of intense sunlight he had the kind of skin that tanned easily. Stupid, *stupid!* because her fingers could feel that skin, fine-grained, taut over muscles and sinews, and she trembled with a desire that weakened every resolution she had made.

When he reached the rocks he hauled himself up and walked across to stare up at the house. Without volition Faine stepped back from the window. He wore no swimsuit and apparently had no shame about being watched, for he shook his head and then ran his hand over his hair, before stretching with sleek animal suppleness. The sun's rays turned him into a gilded statue like something out of Greece's Golden Age, perfect muscles, strength and grace personified. For a long moment Faine watched as he walked back along the reef and stood staring out into the shimmering silver and green expanse of water that formed the estuary. Then he lifted his arms and dived in, body meeting the sea in a clean arc, without splash or fuss.

When he arrived back at the house, clothed, she was glad to see, in a towelling robe, the agreeable smell of perking coffee was everywhere, and she was showered and dressed in a sun-frock and sandals, as crisp as the day.

'Enjoy your swim?' she asked calmly, determined not to allow herself to be affected by that very potent masculinity.

'Marvellous.' Roaming her face, the light hard gaze suddenly sharpened before becoming hooded. 'You should have come in.'

She smiled. 'I hate to admit it, but I like the temperature to be in the high eighties before I dip my toe in.'

'Good God, I've married a sybarite!' he exclaimed, raking a hand through his hair to push it back from his face. 'Don't you know that the sea now is as warm as it's going to be for the whole year? It's only the air which is cooler than in high summer.'

'My brain knows it, but so far it hasn't been able to convince my body.' Faine said, then wished she hadn't, because he immediately surveyed her from her narrow feet to the top of her head, as if imagining her without her clothes.

It was a deliberate attempt to intimidate her and normally it would have succeeded. But she held his glance steadily, refusing to give in to the embarrassment he provoked.

Obviously he was not going to make things easier for her. No doubt he felt as though she had cheated him.

Without thinking she said. 'Burke, can't we talk things over? You must see how I feel—that I can't— that . . .' Under his cool ironic stare her voice faded away and she flushed, miserably conscious of her lack of armour against him.

'Oh yes,' he said after too long a silence. 'Yes, I understand exactly how you feel. That's the only reason I'm prepared to go along with you, for the moment, anyway. I presume after you've made me suffer frustration for a suitable length of time you'll be more amenable.'

That cool glance hardened into ruthlessness. 'But listen to me, Faine, and remember this well. I'm not prepared to wait for ever. When I think the time is right I'll take you, and there'll be no protests and no inquests.'

Anger lit the depths of her eyes, turning them into glittering gold gems. 'I am not staying with you,' she said, that instant making up her mind in a swift reaction to his arrogance.

He smiled, not at all pleasantly. 'Yes, you are. If you'd intended leaving you'd have gone last night.'

As she shook her head he reached out and took her hand, his finger touching the rapid shallow pulse at her wrist, his eyes pinning hers in a merciless glance. 'Let us be perfectly honest,' he said with a hard note of sarcasm threading his dark tones. 'The reason we married—the basic reason—is still there. In spite of all that outrage and indignation you want me—and I certainly want you. No——' as she opened her mouth in an angry interruption, 'no, I've listened to enough of your complaints. Face facts, Faine. You married me because I can give you the background you want, and because the first time you saw me you thought to yourself, "I wonder what he's like as a lover," and you imagined——'

He caught her hand as it flashed towards his face and held it in a grip like a vice, his expression cold and purposeful.

'You might have fooled yourself,' he said, turning the words into a jeer, 'but not me. I knew—a man always knows, you idiot. How the hell else do you expect the sexes to get together? I looked at you, wet and flushed and responsive, and visualised you naked in my arms, in my bed.' He shook her wrists, jerking her off balance against him. Instantly his arms closed around her, one hard on her smooth bare shoulders, the other across her hips holding her so that she felt his blatant hunger.

'And that,' he said softly into her ear, 'that, my lovely shrew, is why, when you've salved your pride, you'll surrender. Deny it as loudly and as often as you like, you know bloody well that the chemistry between us is too powerful for you to hold out indefinitely. If what you discovered yesterday had really appalled you so much you'd never have left the house with me. By doing so you admitted to me and tacitly to yourself that you'd stay. And by doing that you made it clear that sooner or later we'll make love.'

Faine bit her lip, trying by sheer willpower to force her racing heartbeat into a steadier pace. Beneath her fingers the old cotton wrap Burke wore rose and fell with the rhythm of his breathing, a little faster than usual. A soft tangle of hair filled the gap between the lapels; she had never been able to understand why some women thought that masculine characteristic sexy, but it took all her self-command not to touch it with her tongue. Colour flared in her cheeks.

'Damn you!' she muttered in a thick choked voice. 'I will not be used as a substitute——'

'Then make me love *you*,' he interrupted, coldly and brutally, and cut off her protests by taking her open mouth with the kind of sexual urgency that made her grab him in case her knees gave way. Not that there was much hope of her collapsing. He held her too tightly for that, his hands cruel on her body, his mouth taking toll, forcing her head back until she gave a sob of protest.

Then he eased the pressure, finding the smooth curve of her throat when she turned her face away from him, her eyes pressed tight shut to hide even from herself the knowledge that he was right. An expert, she thought bitterly, a brilliant psychologist in his way. Gauging her reactions, able to assess exactly what she would do and why, he was able to probe the depths of her mind with skill and precision. Even now, although his desire was riding him hard, he knew precisely what effect his calculated passion was having on her.

Only one secret remained. He had no idea of her stupid, stupid love for him. And never would, she vowed, opening her eyes as he lifted his head.

'Finished?' she asked coldly, trying to pay him back for the insult he had offered.

Something gleamed, dark and cold and ugly, deep within the light eyes. He smiled slowly and with a single swift movement pulled the straps of her sunfrock down her arms, tugging until the bodice slid down beneath her breasts; all the while he watched her face with narrowed glance.

'No,' he said calmly. 'Just remember this. If I chose to I could take you now, here, on the floor, and there's nothing you could do about it.'

'If you do,' she gritted through tightly clenched teeth, 'I'll divorce you so fast you——' She stopped, colour flaring into her cheeks as his hands moved, cupping her breasts, each thumb stroking slowly, sensually downward, until it reached the hard pink nub. She drew a deep breath and lowered her lashes, so shamed that she could no longer meet his sardonic gaze. Against the honey velvet of her skin his hands were dark, their lean strength threatening and exciting as they moved across her body. The splayed fingers were like bars, imprisoning her in the dark power of his magnetism.

'What will you do?' he asked, and bent his head, his intention very obvious.

It was what she needed to break free from this humiliation. She twisted away, dragging up the straps of her dress, and said stonily, 'I meant it, Burke. The thought of being raped terrifies and repels me.'

'Some women enjoy the idea,' he said, and smiled cynically as she began to protest. 'Oh, calm down. Give me some credit for knowing how devious your sex can be!'

'You've had so many women, I suppose,' she snapped.

'No. I'm rather fastidious in my choice of lovers.'

Some foolish compulsion drove her on to sneer, 'So I suppose I should feel honoured.'

'Quite frankly, I don't give a damn how you feel.'

'I know that.'

Burke looked at her for a moment, fighting the desire

to make some tangible expression of his anger before finally smashing a fist into his other hand, jolted out of his normal self-control.

'What the hell are you trying to do?' he demanded savagely. 'I've never hit a woman in my life but, my God, I'm perilously close to it now!'

It gave her a fierce primitive pleasure to watch him fight visibly for command, skin taut over high cheek-bones, his jaw out-thrust and tight, glaring at her as if he could kill her. Let him feel shame of some sort, she thought viciously; he prided himself on his self-pos-session, on the sophisticated mask which had fooled her as it fooled so many others. Well, Libby might have his love, but she would never have seen him as he was now, staring at her as if he would like nothing better than to kill her, his emotions for once open to scrutiny. Like this he was vulnerable. Defiantly she stared back, her eyes unwinking like flat golden jewels in the pallor of her face, enjoying the fact that he was having to fight for control, force himself to breathe slowly and deeply, relax each muscle in his body until at last he said with cold dispassion:

'Don't try that too often, my dear. Games like it are likely to end in pain and humiliation—your pain, and your humiliation.'

And because she had been frightened by that glimpse of his ferocious temper, Faine turned away from him, hiding her fear under a calm face and voice as she said, 'Don't worry, I don't intend to impinge any more than I have to.'

'And what,' he enquired smoothly, 'do you mean by that?'

The coffee was ready. Faine poured out two cups, took them across to the table and sat down, pushing one across to where she had set a place for him.

'Just that the sooner this—this farce is over the better. Until it is, the cooler we keep the better.' She intended to speak with assurance, and it infuriated her to realise that beneath the calm indifference in her voice there had sounded a note of defiance, as though she was still afraid.

Burke came across to the table and sat down, seemingly without any thought for his nakedness beneath the wrap. Faine fixed her eyes on her coffee, fighting down the awareness which made her heart thump suddenly in her breast.

'This farce, as you call it, will be over when you've had your revenge,' he said. 'As for coolness—well, you are a very cool lady. Enjoy it while you can, because you know damned well that it would take me no more than ten minutes to get you into bed.'

For a moment her fingers tightened around the handle of her cup as she fought the impulse to hurl the contents at him. Humiliation burned corrosively along her veins. In a voice totally lacking emotion she said, 'Well, why don't you, then?'

'Because,' he said deliberately, 'that would really give you cause for a grudge. The decision will be yours, my sweet, so that you can't complain that I took you against your will. You'll come to me when you can't bear the hunger any longer, but until then I'll leave you alone.'

'I think I'd rather you raped me than know that I'm standing in for Libby,' she said harshly, unable to hide her bitterness.

He sighed and his face hardened. 'If it gives you more confidence I'll say your name every five seconds while we're making love.'

Colour flooded her skin, then ebbed, leaving her pale and exhausted. In a defeated voice she said, 'Why won't you let me go, Burke? You don't want me, and I . . . and I . . .'

'And you don't want me,' he finished for her. He reached out and took her hands. She let them lie listlessly in his grasp. 'But you do, don't you, Faine? You see, you can't lie to me, not even for pride's sake. And I want you. I could prove that to you now. I probably should; it would be one thing out of the way. But you'd resent it, and God knows, I don't want that.'

'What do you want?'

He hesitated a moment before saying slowly, 'I want a marriage. I want children and a kind, stimulating, passionate wife. I want laughter and ease and the mental affinity that makes our relationship interesting and exciting. I know that I can make you happy if you'll only let me.'

'And I?' she asked huskily. 'Can I make you happy, when you love Libby and she loves you?'

His fingers tightened on hers. 'Are you worried about my fidelity? I can promise that there's no need. I've had affairs, but not as many as I'm credited with.' A cynical smile invited her response. 'I've never seduced anyone in my life and have been known to go without making love for months at a time.'

Faine bit her lip, bending her head so that he could see only the warm amber crown of her hair. 'You didn't answer my question.'

Silence, and then he said deliberately, 'Yes, I think you will make me happy. What I feel for Libby is——'

'It doesn't matter,' she interrupted, afraid now that she had forced him to speak of his emotions. She did not want him to describe just what he felt for Libby—

it hurt too much. 'It doesn't matter. I had no right to——'

'Oh, I think you have. After all, you are my wife.' His voice invested the last word with an irony which made her go pale and try to pull her hands away.

Instantly his grip tightened as if it pleased him to hurt her. She had forced the issue out into the open, but although his touch and his voice both revealed latent cruelty he would never know just how painful it was for her.

'I don't believe in waste,' he said, smoothing the skin over the tiny blue veins at her wrists. 'There was no future for Libby and me, none at all. Gavin has her complete loyalty and I respect her for her decision. Even if she had been willing to leave him for me I doubt if I'd have taken her. I love my brother and the protective habits of years are almost impossible to break. And my grandmother—well, I needn't tell you how she would have reacted.'

'No.' Ellen Guilford was a darling, very modern in her outlook, but her reactions were deeply rooted in the conventions of her childhood. To her, duty and self-control were more than concepts, they were guide posts to live by. She would have been grievously shocked and hurt had Burke taken Gavin's wife for himself.

'I know how you feel,' he said drily, releasing her. He knew, of course; in spite of his disclaimer about his sexual prowess he was experienced enough to realise when her anger had died. He probably understood her better than she understood herself—witness his clever, calculating pursuit of her.

But he did not—never would—know that she loved him with all her heart and her soul and her body.

Faine lifted her head slightly but refused to meet his glance. Oh, she would have to be so careful! Burke thought it was a desire for security and the physical and mental affinity between them which would keep her in this marriage. He must never know the truth, because she didn't think her pride could bear it. It was then that she realised that she had decided to stay with him.

Slowly, carefully, she drank some coffee, then asked, 'And how do I feel?'

'You told me,' he retorted, a hard note in the deep voice. 'Betrayed. At first I thought it a very dramatic word for you to use, but I'd forgotten your pride. I can understand how the discovery affected you.'

Anger began to burn deep within her. Her gaze lifted as in a voice that was crisp and clear she asked, 'And just how would you have felt, had the situation been reversed?'

Her question startled him, arrested whatever he had been going to say. For a moment he stared at her, then his lips twisted as he said deliberately, 'I'd have been bloody angry. But I'd not have walked out. I'd have taken you, stamped my brand on you so firmly that you'd never have broken free. And after that,' with a look that stripped her clothes from her, 'I'd have kept you too busy to be pining after a lost love.'

Almost she pointed out the fundamental difference between a man's reaction and a woman's, but if she did he would know her secret. A man could make love without feeling more than desire, but most women invested considerable emotional capital in a relationship. Passion was important, but without love any relationship was ultimately sterile.

'Obviously we look at things from different angles,'

she said carefully. 'I don't have that kind of confidence.'

Silence, but somehow the tension had eased. Sunlight blazed across the polished floor, was caught in tiny sparks in the cutlery, glittered around a cut glass beaker full of orange juice. For the first time in days Faine felt hungry.

'Perhaps time will give it to you,' said Burke, and lifted her hand and kissed it. 'I meant what I said,' he told her quietly, holding her gaze with his own. 'I'm sure that I can make you happy—and that you can make me just as happy. Otherwise I wouldn't have married you. In time we'll make this a real marriage, one that will stand any test. Until then, let's take it one day at a time, shall we?'

CHAPTER NINE

AND that was exactly what they did. The week of that strange honeymoon passed so quickly that ever afterwards, looking back on it, Faine could never separate the days. Like watercolours on wet paper they ran together, a muted panorama of sun and sea and sand. Slowly, without realising how easy it was, she relaxed. The first time that Burke sought her hand as they walked along the hard wet beach below the high tide mark she flinched away, but he refused to allow her to avoid him.

'No,' he said coolly, capturing her fingers. 'I'm not an ogre and I refuse to be treated as one.'

And because her love weakened her she allowed the small intimacy while her brain was telling her that she was every kind of fool.

What made it worse was that she knew exactly what he was doing. Skilfully, cleverly, making his moves with all the dedication of a professional chess player, he was backing her into a corner from which there would be only one escape. And when it came he would be there, and Faine knew now that when he finally forced the issue she would not refuse him. Not even her pride had any power over the frustrated sexuality that held her in thrall.

Oh, she managed to hide the hunger that gnawed at her, cloaking it with the serene good humour which had been part of the persona she had made for herself, the mask which prevented too close an inspection of her real personality. Essentially reserved, made even more so by the death of her parents and Dougal's defection, she was galled that Burke should have seen beneath that cool restraint to the passionate, responsive person who was hidden there. Accepting his own virility, he had known that he needed a woman of equal sensuality to meet and match him. And she had fallen into his hand like a ripe peach.

Driving back to Auckland, she stared through the windscreen on to the lovely coastal scenery of hills and bays, little rivers and patches of bush, and wondered just how he had known that she would go up in flames for him. Instinct, she decided, the same instinct which had warned her that he was dangerous. Somehow he had recognised the latent sexuality beneath the calm surface and once he had assured himself of that all that was necessary was to see if their tastes and minds meshed.

Which they did, very much so. His quick cold intelligence struck sparks from her brain; this week they had argued and agreed, finding pleasure in the swift interchange of ideas and thoughts. Even their pleasure in simple things was similar; they had tramped over the hills and sat for hours saying very little, watching the ever-changing panorama of the estuary. Once, caught by rain, Burke had contrived a shelter and showed her how to make a fire using dry sticks and a bow, laughing at her incredulity when the tinder finally caught fire.

'Clever!' she teased, and he had grinned and said, 'Oh, I believe in being prepared for any eventuality.'

You do indeed, Faine thought drily. He was totally reliable, the kind of person one would trust always to know what to do.

Oddly—and perversely—this aspect of his character made her bristle. Sitting beside him in the car, she admitted that just once she would dearly like to see him in a situation he couldn't control.

And then she thought of Libby locked in his arms and felt the familiar nausea clog her throat.

It wasn't *fair*! They had so much in common, so much going for them, yet over everything was the spectre of Libby with her lovely anguished face, her loyalty to a man who enjoyed hurting her, the silken noose she had wound around Burke's heart.

Faine turned her head and stared sightlessly out of the side window. Damn Libby, she thought fiercely, driven by an agony of need, damn her to hell! Why hadn't she left Gavin and gone to Burke? At least then two people would have been happy and Burke would never have gone looking for a wife to keep him out of temptation's way.

And Faine Harding, wife in name only, would still be Faine Hellier, heart-whole and contented with the placid tenor of her life.

But at the thought of never having known him she bit her lip and, unaware, advanced a little further along the path to complete surrender. She could not be sorry. However much Burke had hurt her, and he would never know how much, she was glad that she loved him. Whatever happened in the future which seemed so bleak and unsure, she would be the richer for having known him.

'You're looking very fierce,' he commented, touching the tightly clasped hands in her lap.

It took an effort to summon up a smile, but she managed it. 'I'm looking forward to getting into the garden,' she returned.

'You'd better advertise for someone to do the heavy work for you.' Burke smiled as she turned deliberate eyes on to his wide shoulders and strongly muscled arms. 'No, my dear. I enjoy gardens, but I intend to relax in mine. And that doesn't involve digging it.'

His idea of relaxation, she discovered in the weeks that followed, was half an hour spent swimming each morning and a vigorous game of squash three times a week. No wonder he was as lean and fit as an athlete. He worked long hours, but apparently had developed the skill of delegating, for each day he was home early enough to spend the long, golden evening with her.

Strangely enough Faine was happy. On the surface, anyway, and even deeper than that, in some part of her which had been starved since her parents had died. With Burke there was total security—exactly what he thought she had married for. Her talent for home-making gave her immense satisfaction as she worked each day in the house, polishing and cleaning, choosing the perfect fittings to bring it back to perfection. The expert Burke had suggested to help her was a woman of forty or so with an intuitive feel for old houses and a seeing eye when it came to discerning the potential of old furniture no matter how many layers of grime and cobwebs covered it. Life in a house with the decorators in was not exactly easy, but they managed, Burke showing a surprising ease at accommodating himself to ladders and dust sheets.

At least it meant that what little entertaining they did was at restaurants where it was easy to maintain the smooth façade of their marital happiness. And by living on the spot Faine could spend many hours in the garden with the sturdy youth who had answered her advertisement. He knew nothing about gardening, but he intended to learn and he was proud of his strength. Faine had thought she would miss the library and her work; instead, she found her days so busy that she barely thought of her old life.

It was all a front, of course. At the end of each day when she closed the door of her bedroom the devils were let loose. All sorts, she thought wryly, lust and anger, jealousy and pride, a hideous complexity of emotions which kept her awake every night into the small hours, burning with an intolerable desire. Each morning she made up carefully, hiding the ravages of the night, but Burke knew. Those pale eyes missed nothing, and when he kissed her, which he did on leaving and returning to the house, it was with the sure knowledge that the impersonal touch of his mouth brought her to flaming life. Yet he did not pursue his advantage, making it quite clear that he wanted nothing less than complete capitulation.

At times she hated him for his arrogance, the inbuilt self-confidence that assured him that her surrender was only a matter of time. The ruthlessness which allowed him to wait for her to make the first move repelled her, but each day that passed deepened and strengthened her love.

And then the house was finished, miraculously, it seemed.

'Invite the family to dinner,' said Burke, sitting back into a lounger on the brick terrace.

It was an order delivered with a total lack of expression. Faine nodded. 'Of course,' she returned. 'Do you mind if I ask Margot Forsyth? She's worked so hard. If it hadn't been for her everything would have taken much longer.'

'Good idea.' He lifted his glass in salute. 'Why not see if the others who helped can't come too? Sandy Greenfield and Bill Turner.'

He was referring to the architect and the builder who had handled the renovations. Did he realise that she didn't want an intimate party, with Libby the only focus of Burke's interest? Probably. He was so *bloody* astute, she thought wearily, draining the last of the lime juice in her glass.

Since the wedding they had seen very little of Libby and Gavin, not much more of Ellen. His grandmother was every bit as astute as Burke, so she must have known how things were between him and Libby; almost certainly that was why she had promoted this marriage so enthusiastically. She would have decided that the best way of breaking the stranglehold Libby had on his heart was a passionate wife, and then to make sure that he and his sister-in-law met as little as possible.

And Libby, of course—well, jealous and envious though she was, Faine could not help feeling sorry for her. Burke's marriage must have added to the hell in which she lived; she would not be eager to see him with his new wife. She could not know, of course, just how empty his marriage was.

'I'll see if I can organise a date,' said Faine getting to her feet. 'So close to Christmas, most of them will probably be booked out.'

But they weren't, and they accepted, and they came, all bearing gifts for the new house. Libby looked enchanting, thinner, more fragile than ever, her ethereal beauty haunting and beckoning. Gavin seemed to take a malicious delight in tormenting her; Faine didn't dare to watch Burke for any indication of how his brother's behaviour affected him, but so aware of him was she that she sensed the tension behind the suave mask.

And when they had gone she heard him in his room walking the floor, and her heart ached. Next day he left before she woke. A call from his secretary informed her that he would be eating out with clients; it was after midnight when he came home, and even then he did not go to bed. For an hour Faine lay listening to his movements, then she got up and pulled on a dressing gown and went into his bedroom.

Burke was sitting on the side of his bed, elbows on his knees, his hands supporting his head. For the first time Faine saw him defeated, his proud head bowed in a pain too deep for expression.

'You should be in bed,' she said huskily, touching his shoulder in a brief compassionate movement. 'You didn't sleep last night.'

He lifted his head, staring at her as though he had never seen her before, the pale depths of his eyes darkening. 'No,' he said after a moment. 'No, I didn't. How did you know?'

'I heard you.' She bit her lip, lowering her lashes so that he couldn't see the emotions behind their thick screen.

'I'm sorry. I'll take a sleeping pill tonight.'

Faine shook her head impatiently. 'It didn't matter, although I agree you should try to get some rest.' She hesitated, for he was looking at her with an odd, blank stare that made her uneasy. 'Burke, is there anything I can do . . .'

Her voice trailed away into silence, for he smiled and stood up. She took an involuntary step backwards, impelled away from him by the set purpose which hardened the strong features into ruthlessness.

'Burke . . .?'

That smile lingered, merciless, totally cynical. 'As it happens,' he said deliberately catching hold of her wrist, 'there is something you can do for me. You can give me the best remedy for sleeplessness in the world.'

Impossible to pretend that she did not know what he meant. He did not attempt to hide the hunger in his eyes as they rested for a moment on the quick rise and fall of her breast, then roamed upwards the length of her throat to rest with insolent lustfulness on her pale lips before meeting the appeal of her glance.

'I'm tired,' he said harshly, jerking her towards him, 'tired of so many things. I want to forget for a little while.'

'I won't be used!' she exclaimed, pushing against his chest.

'Oh, yes, you will. Well and truly used.' His fingers tightened on her wrists. Without much effort he separated her hands, forced them behind her back, levering her against the length of his body in an embrace from which she could not free herself. His mouth was an inch from hers, so close that his breath warmed her lips as he said implacably, 'I'm not going to beg any more, Faine, or wait until it pleases you to stop punishing me. I need you now.'

'So you'll rape me.' She stared at the taut line of his jaw, afraid to lift her eyes in case he saw how his nearness affected her.

The corner of his mouth lifted in a sardonic smile. 'Don't be naïve,' he said against her temple. 'Just relax.'

She fought him until he lost patience and used his great strength to subdue her. Then she stood rigid in his arms, refusing to let her body respond to his practised seduction, her eyes unfocussed as she stared straight in front of her.

He became angry, the pale sea-green of his gaze darkening to turbulence as he forced her face up to meet the harsh ardour of his kiss.

'Kiss me, damn you,' he muttered roughly against her mouth.

She shook her head, as angry as he—more angry, for beneath the anger there was excitement, and she was repelled by the knowledge that she could be aroused by his brutality. Yet aroused she was, her body beginning to thrill with a heat he was too experienced not to recognise.

Sure enough he laughed, a mere ghost of a sound without any amusement in it, and taunted, 'Still salving your pride? O.K., if that's the way you want it——'

His hands moved, there was a ripping sound and she gasped, looking in astonished horror at the wreck of her dressing gown on the floor. For a moment she was too shocked at his sudden violence to remember that she had only a very flimsy nightgown on.

'No——' she stammered, hugging her arms across her breasts in a vain attempt to ward him off.

'Then take it off,' he said. 'If you like it that much. I don't feel inclined to be gentle.'

'You—you said you wouldn't . . .' She stepped backwards, swallowing nervously. 'You can't rape me!'

Burke laughed again, and reached out to run a finger from her mouth to the hollow between her breasts. Colour bloomed in Faine's cheeks; she breathed in quickly and sharply, fighting her desire to give in. Defiantly she tightened her arms, then flushed again as the pressure pushed her breasts together, almost entrapping his finger.

'But you want me to,' he said softly, enjoying her discomfiture. 'You know, I'd heard that there were women who enjoyed being raped but never believed it. Incredible to find myself married to one!'

As she opened her mouth to refute his statement he pulled her hands from beneath her armpits, pinioned her wrists together with one hand and forced them above her head, then with the other hand jerked her nightgown up. Faine gasped and kicked at him, writhed frantically trying to get free. The next moment she found herself spreadeagled on the bed, halfsobbing her frustration as he held her there with a hand and knee while he removed his dressing gown and came down beside her, his determination to take her so plain that she no longer struggled.

'You're beautiful,' he said softly, sliding his hand beneath her back to arch her towards him. 'Skin like cream and hair like honey and a body made for pleasure.' His mouth traced the long line of her throat, biting the fine skin gently.

Sheer shock kept Faine still. She should have known that Burke would not follow any well-worn conventions in lovemaking, but she had so little experience herself on which to base any comparisons that she did not know whether the subtle pleasure of his teeth against her skin was a normal reaction, or whether she felt like this because it was Burke who was making love to her.

His taunt about her enjoying a rape kept her still; only much later it occurred to her that that could have been his reason for making it. If so it revealed how well he knew women, but by then she did not need to be convinced of that. Experience showed.

He knew exactly how to pleasure her, using his hands and his voice and his mouth as the means of her seduction until finally she signified her surrender with a shuddering sigh as she nuzzled her mouth into his throat.

Afterwards, still in his arms but far from sleep, she listened to the soft sound of his breath and knew that she loved him far, far more than she had ever believed she could love. The emotions Dougal had roused paled into nothing; even the way she had felt for Burke when she married him was insignificant compared to the overwhelming surge of emotion, deep and true, which held her in its grip now.

She smiled, thinking with a sardonic lack of humour that he was capable of wresting from her far more than she was prepared to give freely. First her love, unwanted and unrequited, and then a passionate response that had shocked her by its shameless intensity. It was as though another woman lived within her, a wanton creature intent on satisfying desires the staid librarian had only ever read about. And then with a strong suspicion that such things were the febrile results of overheated imaginations!

Well, she knew better now. In spite of his threat Burke had been gentle with her until her increasing desire had swept away her shyness in a flood of sensation that hungered for the satisfaction that only their complete union could give her.

Her ardour had surprised him into soft laughter so that, angry with herself and him, she had bitten his shoulder, and then he had not been gentle any longer, stamping his brand on her body as he had once threatened to with a fire and arrogance that wrung from her an intensity of stimulation so unbearable that when he groaned her name she barely heard him, lost in the voluptuous reactions he had roused in her.

But she had not told him of her love, and afterwards, when he lay with his head at her breast, she was glad, for he said, 'If I'd realised what I was waiting for I might not have been so patient.'

He paused, but when she said nothing, too honest to demur but refusing to admit that he sent her up in flames, he continued, 'First time, Faine?'

'Does it matter?'

'No.' He moved, pulling her close so that she lay against him, warm, exhausted by the special demands that complete surrender made on the body and yet, oddly, completely relaxed.

'No, it doesn't matter,' he said lazily into her hair. 'Perhaps I would have been a little more gentle, although I doubt it. Your response was enough to make me forget any resolutions I might have made. I must admit to being surprised.'

A wave of heat scorched through her body. That she could be so shameless was a shock to her; she had thought that for a woman making love meant following where one's lover led, but she had astounded herself by the fierce demands of her body and her total abandonment to them.

'Why?' she asked huskily, afraid that he found her ardour distasteful.

'Oh, I'd somehow gained the impression that you'd had some experience. You've been engaged. I know that sleeping with your intended isn't universal, but from what I've heard it must be almost.'

'Not for me,' Faine said stiffly. 'He didn't——' She stopped precipitately, afraid to admit even to herself that no one but Burke made her lose every inhibition.

'He didn't what? Try? I refuse to believe that.' He laughed beneath his breath and slid a hand up to her chin, tilting her head back against his arm so that he could see her face. 'No normal man would resist the sort of temptation you offer, especially not if you wore his ring.'

Faine moved restlessly; the room was lit only by the moon so that their intertwined forms were washed in a cool silver glow that glamourised even as it revealed. She had been glad when Burke switched off the lights, for her shyness with him had lasted until his practised lovemaking had swept it away. Now, looking up into his face, she noted the glinting mockery beneath his lashes as his glance became openly possessive, and realised that for him making love bathed in moonlight had a glamour of its own. For her, too.

'Well, we didn't,' she said, stiffly.

'Mm.' Burke touched her ear gently, his finger exploring the delicate whorls and convolutions, strangely erotic. He smiled as she drew a sharp breath and his hand moved to her throat and then to the tender curves of her breast.

Faine moved uneasily, aware that the desire she had thought slaked was beginning to burn again within her.

'You're beautiful,' he told her softly. 'Even in this moonlight you're honey-coloured ... sweet as honey ... One of these days we'll make love in the sun ... you'll glow like a tawny rose in my arms ...'

Seduced by the magical quality of his voice and words, she lifted her hand to press it against the faintly roughened skin of his cheek. He laughed and shaped the contours of her body, his hand sweeping slowly across her skin, lingering, teasing and tormenting until she arched against him, the movement involuntary.

'What is it?' he asked. 'What do you want?'

He would not touch her until she told him and showed him. Then he smiled, and this time it was slower, infinitely slower, and she discovered that there were degrees of ecstasy and that so far she had only scaled the foothills.

When her heart resumed its normal beat he kissed her, a gentle, tender kiss, and said softly, 'Sleep now. It's late.'

But she lay long after his breathing had regularised into the deep even pace of unconsciousness, her eyes closed but her mind active. Why, why had he chosen tonight to make their marriage real? There could be only one reason. Tormented by Libby's presence in their house, he had sublimated his love by taking his recalcitrant wife.

Tomorrow she would be humiliated by the fact that he had used her to slake the fire which had been set

alight by another woman, but for tonight she could
only wonder at the ecstasy his body had given her.
Often and often she had read that for a woman love for
the first time was nothing much, that it took time and
a tender, thoughtful lover to arouse her to her full potential.

Perhaps she was different. Her own sensuality
almost frightened her, yet she could not be sorry for it;
Burke had led her into complete abandonment with
such erotic enjoyment that she could only be glad that
she was able to give him this release. At least, for a
time, she had not thought of Libby and his hopeless
love.

Yawning, she moved against him, smiled as his arm
immediately tightened across her waist. Just for this
night, just for now, in this dreamy time before sleep,
she would pretend that they were lovers in the true
sense of the term.

CHAPTER TEN

PERHAPS she should have had some sort of premonition;
but when the telephone rang at midday the next day
she lifted the receiver without any fears.

It was Burke's secretary, with a note in her usually
modulated tones that made Faine uneasy.

'Mrs Harding? Oh, Mrs Harding, Mr Harding asked
me to ring you to . . .' the crisp voice faded as the
woman took a deep breath, 'to tell you that he's been
called to the hospital. His brother—Mr Gavin

Harding—is there. He—he's had an accident.' Silence, then the little voice asked anxiously, 'Mrs Harding? Are you——?'

'Yes—yes.' Faine noted that the knuckles of her hand were white as the fingers clenched on the edge of the table. 'What hospital?'

'Auckland.'

'How—how badly is he hurt?'

A short silence, as though she was trying to soften a blow before she said baldly, 'I think—he's dead, Mrs Harding.'

'I see.'

Another silence while Faine tried to force her whirling thoughts into some sort of order.

The secretary asked diffidently, 'Mrs Harding, shall I order you a taxi?'

Would he want her there? Faine bit her lip until it hurt. 'Yes,' she said at last in a voice that was totally blank. 'Yes, thank you.'

It was unfortunate that she should walk into the waiting room at the hospital at the exact time that Libby broke down, for it afforded her an excellent view of her husband enfolding his sister-in-law in his arms, his expression set in lines of such bitter anger that the blood drained from Faine's skin, leaving her cold and clammy.

'Don't,' he said heavily, not seeing beyond Libby's lovely, anguished face. 'I beg of you, don't cry, Libby.'

'I c—can't—I can't——'

From the depths of her own agony Faine summoned up the strength to go towards them; it hurt so much that she never after remembered just what she said, but within a few moments she was supporting the weeping Libby while Burke took his grandmother's arm. Ellen Guilford seemed to have shrunk, but although there were tears in her eyes she stood erect as Burke spoke to someone from the hospital about the arrangements that had to be made.

The following hours were nightmarish. Libby collapsed completely and had to be put to bed. After a visit from the doctor a sedative lulled her off to sleep. Ellen stayed with her until she was deeply unconscious, then came to where Faine stood in the French window of the little sitting room, staring out across the lawn.

'Is she asleep?'

'Yes.' Ellen sat down, her face drawn and pale, suddenly old. 'Where's Burke?'

'In the study. He's talking to a policeman.'

Tears sprang to the older woman's eyes. Her mouth worked silently for a few moments, then she said harshly, 'It's probably the best thing that could have happened, but oh, I will miss him so!'

And she wept, clinging to Faine's hands as if they were a lifeline.

A long time later Faine brought her a damp flannel and a towel to mop up, and poured her brandy and some for herself. Since they had been home the telephone had rung almost continually, but the housekeeper was there answering it, taking messages with calm efficiency.

Faine sipped her brandy, forcing her mind to deal only with the immediate problems. Later, when she was alone, would be soon enough to worry about other aspects of Gavin's death.

Both women's glances flew towards the door as Burke came through, his expression bleak and remote. His eyes rested on Faine, chilling her with their total lack of expression, then moved to his grandmother's ravaged face.

'My dear,' he said roughly, and went across to where she sat, his handsome face set in lines of cold restraint.

Ellen put out her hand. He took it and bent to kiss her cheek.

'My poor darling,' she whispered, and it was impossible to decide which of her grandsons she referred to.

Burke straightened up and walked across to a chair, lowering himself into it with a sigh.

'Is that brandy?' he asked, closing his eyes. 'Pour me some, Faine, will you?'

He emptied the glass in one gulp, still with his eyes closed. Faine went quietly back to her vigil at the window.

'What happened?' Ellen asked on a dragging note.

'He swerved to avoid a child who ran out into the road, and the car hit a power pole before it went over a forty-foot bank. The child's mother saw it all.' He spoke without expression, his voice drained of colour and emotion.

'I see.' Ellen bowed her head, passing a hand over her eyes. 'Poor Gavin,' she whispered, 'poor, poor Gavin. What—what arrangements have you made, Burke?'

He told her, still in that same empty voice.

There was a long silence before Ellen asked, 'And what about that poor child in there, Burke? What will happen to her?'

Faine ached for him to make some acknowledgment of her presence, but he didn't even bother to look her way as he answered, 'She'll be taken care of, don't worry. Have you had anything to eat?'

'I couldn't.' Ellen's distress was real and immediate, but he ignored it, opening his eyes to look at her.

'You'll have to,' he said bluntly, 'or you'll collapse. And God knows, darling, we need you now.'

Faine set her glass down on a table, saying quietly, 'I'll see to it.'

'Good girl.' But he spoke absently, as though she had no reality for him.

Perhaps she hadn't. As she worked in the kitchen she found herself thinking bitterly that last night might never have happened. Those exquisite minutes spent in his arms meant nothing to him now that Libby needed him. Her guilt and her grief combined to tie him even closer to her.

But that was a forbidden direction for Faine's thoughts to take. Not yet while these few days were still to be endured.

Endured was the correct word. Ellen Guilford called on her considerable reserves of strength to see her through, but Libby's collapse was dramatic and complete, forcing her to spend most of her time in bed under sedation. Faine found herself taking over more of the decisions, which left Ellen to find some ease of spirit and comfort in helping the housekeeper with everyday tasks which had to be done, tragedy or no tragedy.

It rained during the funeral service, but at the graveside the sun shone brightly. Libby wept, leaning heavily on Burke's arm, barely able to retain her slender grip on her composure even though heavily tranquillised. She looked like a wraith, a beautiful, ravaged ghost with the eyes of a tortured child, imprisoned in a hell from which nothing and nobody could rescue her. Her anguish aroused Faine's protective instincts; like every other person who spoke to Gavin's widow she treated her with a gentleness that made the tears well and spill from those enormous blue eyes.

Now, as the minister's solemn voice intoned the final phrases, she collapsed against Burke, fighting desperately for some kind of composure. The slender body curved against him, relying on his strength and steadiness; instantly his arm circled her trembling shoulders protectively. Ellen turned to Faine, an agonised entreaty in her eyes. Obeying the unspoken command, Faine moved, taking Libby's hand in hers.

Not here, not in front of the crowd of mourners, Ellen had pleaded silently. Let there be no scandal. It was perhaps symptomatic of the era in which she had grown up that even through her grief she had ensured that there was no scope for rumours of any sort. Certainly Libby was grief-stricken enough to satisfy the most cynical.

Faine flinched, betrayed by bitterness into such an unworthy thought. Whatever emotion Libby was gripped by, and some of it had to be guilt, she was suffering and deserved only sympathy.

Burke's glance across the bent black head was an imperative summons. She nodded, stepping back to take Ellen's arm as they turned away from the grave.

Poor Gavin, so young and so doomed, at last at peace. Had he known what his wife felt for the brother he both loved and resented? No one would ever know now.

Back at the house there was the usual subdued gathering, most of whom stayed only a few minutes before leaving. Libby was back in bed, exhausted and shivering with reaction until sleep claimed her.

Faine moved quietly through the room, acting as a

subsidiary hostess while keeping an alert eye on Ellen. At least the older woman seemed to be comforted by the condolences offered her; that strength she shared with her grandson kept her erect, but there was colour in her cheeks now and once or twice she smiled.

Almost impossible to guess how Burke felt! Unless you were his wife, who loved him. Dominant and implacable, he stood, his handsome face aloof as he spoke to his guests. He's hating this, Faine thought drearily. He was loathing every minute, each person and all the softly-spoken sympathy. For a moment she stood helpless beneath a pain fiercer far than any she had known before, divining with that curious extra-sensory perception her love had given her that the reason for his tension lay sobbing in her sleep only a few yards away.

At last it was over. Burke turned to Faine, looking at her with the cold lack of interest he had treated her to since Gavin's death.

'I'm needed at the office,' he said. 'Don't wait dinner for me.'

'Do you—are we going to spend tonight here too?'

The dark sweep of his lashes hid whatever emotion there was in his eyes. His mouth hardened. 'Yes,' he answered.

Faine said nothing, but one hand, the one out of his sight, clenched.

After a moment he said evenly, 'I can't leave Ellen by herself to cope with Libby. You go home if you want to.'

'No, I'll stay.'

They slept in separate bedrooms here, joined by a connecting door which hadn't been opened once.

Faine gave a fleeting look upwards. Burke's features

were impassive, as hard as a mask carved of teak. It was at that moment that Faine gave up all hope. All the things they shared, the astringent companionship, the sexual harmony, the same sense of humour—they meant nothing compared to the overwhelming passion Libby aroused in him.

Ice settled in her heart, numbing it. 'I'll keep some dinner for you,' she said in a voice totally devoid of warmth and life, and turned away before he could see just what he had done to her.

'Faine.'

She stopped, but did not look back.

'Thank you for being such a tower of strength.' The words were conventional, but there was a bitter note beneath them that made her close her eyes in momentary anguish.

'It was nothing,' she said harshly, and walked away from him, walked away from love and warmth and laughter to a future that was bleak indeed.

Later that night, awake in her bed, she heard him come in and eased herself over to look at the clock. Two o'clock! Poor Burke, driven by God knew what demons to work like a demon himself.

When all was silent she lay on her back, hands behind her head, staring across the quietly luxurious room to where a fuzzy haze of light against the curtains denoted the moon. Sleep had never been so elusive, yet she was exhausted, her eyelids heavy and sticky with tiredness while the same few thoughts chased themselves around her brain.

How was she going to get through the next few weeks? Very painfully, she thought with anguish. To leave Burke now would give rise to the scandal which Ellen so feared, yet surely it was too much to expect her to stay and watch him with Libby, now free? Ellen could not be so cruel!

Sighing, she admitted that strength was not the only thing Burke had inherited from his grandmother. Ellen was ruthless enough to demand such a sacrifice, and Faine knew that she was fond enough of the older woman—and so much in love with Burke—that she would stay.

Ironic beyond calculation that Burke thought she had married for security! What security had there been for her with Libby a constant threat? It was a hard lesson to learn, that stability could only come from within. By now, she thought sardonically, she should have learnt it well. The death of her parents had been the first time she had been confronted with it; Dougal's betrayal the clincher. Yet she had come back for more. Perhaps she had at last been convinced. From now on she would grow an armour over her heart and nothing, not ever again, would pierce it.

The tears she had denied for so long began to flow. She turned, crushing them into the pillow, her slender body racked and torn with a pain she dared not reveal.

'*Faine!*'

Burke's voice choked her into terrified silence; her hands clenched convulsively on to the pillow.

He sat down on the side of the bed and tried to gather her into his arms, but she resisted, turning her head away, her body stiff and awkward in his grasp.

'My dear,' he said painfully, the deep voice coloured by some dark emotion, 'don't fight me—please.'

I can't bear it. I can't *bear* it. For a moment she thought she had spoken aloud. Her whole body tensed in a spasm of rejection as he touched her shoulder. His hand was gentle as it moved beneath the heavy tossed curls to the nape of her neck, gentle and tender as he began to massage the tight muscles.

'Do you know *Romeo and Juliet* at all?' he asked after long moments.

She did not trust her voice, so nodded, a quick jerk of her head.

'Somewhere in it Juliet says: *'O! I have bought the mansion of a love But not possessed it.'* I've done that to you, haven't I? Useless to say now that I'm sorry.'

Still she couldn't speak and still his hand kept up the smooth rhythmic movement across her shoulders and neck. Strange that there should be such an erotic charge to so comforting a gesture!

'Better?'

She nodded again, lifting herself free. Much more of that and she would be pleading with him to continue— and that sort of humiliation she did not need.

'I suppose everything caught up with me,' she offered, her voice thick and husky as she turned to face him.

The room was very dark. All that she could see was his darker shape against the window.

'You've been wonderful. Ellen told me that she wouldn't have been able to cope if you hadn't been here to help.'

For a moment Faine's teeth clamped down on her bottom lip so hard that tomorrow it would be swollen. Then she said coolly, 'I'm glad I was able to help. Burke, what do we do now?'

His head turned. 'What do you mean?'

'You know exactly what I mean.'

A slight pause, then he said tonelessly, 'Nothing. We go on as we are.'

So that was it! Some bitter loyalty kept him from

making the break. Faine wasn't even tempted.

'No,' she said harshly. 'I'm disappointed in you. You should know me well enough by now to realise that I won't stand in your way.'

'We're married,' he stated with blunt candour. 'I made vows that I intended to keep. I still intend to keep them. You haven't much of an opinion of me if you think I'd jettison you just because circumstances have altered.'

Faine dragged herself upright against the headboard, bringing her knees up beneath the sheet which was all that she had over her. Winding her arms around her knees, she said harshly, 'And you have a very poor opinion of *me* if you think I'm going to keep you to those vows. You should never have made them in the first place, but at least nowadays we aren't forced to abide by them.' She drew a deep breath, made her voice calm and positive, with no sign of the pain she felt. 'Burke, Libby needs you.'

'And you don't?'

Oh, God! How could he be so cruel? Very firmly she answered, 'No.'

'Cool, sophisticated Faine,' he taunted with an underlying note of savage sarcasm. 'I wonder if you realise how bloody provocative that calm, self-contained image you project is?'

She flinched, as much at the unexpected attack as at his hand around her wrist, a long finger pressing the blue vein where her life-beat throbbed.

'Nothing to say?' He laughed without humour deep in his throat. 'Perhaps it's just as well. You may not need me, but you want me, and I haven't forgotten how much ardour you possess when you're aroused.' His voice deepened, became thick. 'You're aroused now, aren't you? That's one thing I've always been able to do to you, make you long to go to bed with me. It amused me the way you tried to hide it beneath that self-assurance you cling to so desperately. Every time I came near you that pulse beat faster——'

'Be quiet!' The words cracked like whips into the still room. Torn by humiliation, Faine wished only to stop the cruel, jeering taunts. Always, *always* she had known there was a dark streak in Burke, and now, God knew why, now it was revealed to her.

It hurt to jerk her wrist free from his grip, but she managed it. Only he laughed again, dangerous, disturbing laughter, and lunged across the bed and slowly, with brutal, inexorable force, dragged her into his lap. Writhing, the breath coming in harsh pants between her lips, she fought him as he grabbed the thin straps of her nightgown and pushed them down, baring her to the waist.

'Burke!' she whimpered, terrified by this frightening desire she could feel in him, this need to degrade her.

He took no notice. One hand held her by her tangle of curls, tipping her head back so that he could watch her, the other moved sensuously across her breasts. Now that her eyes were accustomed to the darkness in the room she could see his expression, and she shuddered with horror at the icy glitter in his eyes.

'Please,' she whispered beneath her breath. 'Don't make me hate you.'

'Why should I care how you feel about me?' The words were thick, as brutal as the long probing fingers on her soft flesh.

Against her skin she could feel the heat from his body, every muscle taut with control, his heart thundering into her shoulder.

'Well?' he asked into her ear. 'Are you going to give me what I want or do I have to hurt you to get it? You know bloody well you'll give in eventually.' He laughed strangely and bit her ear-lobe, hurting her yet exciting her.

'I wonder which is the more dignified, to fight for your honour or lie back and accept my possession as coldly as you can. I doubt if you'll remain in full control of yourself. That's what you hate about me, isn't it? The knowledge that I can reduce you to a mindless wanton, sobbing and pleading for release.'

'I don't hate you,' she moaned, knowing now that there was no way she could stop what was going to happen. Burke's hand moved from her breast to the narrow smooth curve of her waist, then traced the bowl of her hips and down, touching, probing without tenderness, creating fire in her loins. Galvanised into action, she twisted and fought like a madwoman, attacking him with her teeth and nails until he brought her under control and forced her to accept the hard invasion of his body.

And then she was caught up in the blaze of passion she feared, body in complete control, wanting only him, his mouth and his hands, the driving force of his desire to lift her through the spiral of sensation that went on and on, and lasted a century or a second.

She lay exhausted, her head turned into the pillow, while his harsh breathing eased into its normal pattern and strength came back into his body. Slow tears gathered beneath her eyelids; her throat ached with their suppression. Burke lifted himself from her and sat on the side of the bed, head in his hands.

'Dear God,' he breathed, an immense tiredness dulling his voice. 'You drive me insane!'

'I'm going,' she told him harshly. 'Tomorrow.'

He turned, took her listless hand and pressed it against his mouth. 'I'm sorry,' he said quietly. 'God, will I never finish giving you reasons to hate me! Is there any chance of your becoming pregnant?'

'No.' She had made sure of that, visiting the doctor before their marriage—no doubt because of that same warning instinct which had tried so hard to prevent their marriage. In future, she thought viciously, she was going to listen very carefully to these instincts— they seemed to have a far better knowledge of what was going on than her brain.

'I meant what I said,' Burke told her wearily. 'I don't want you to go, Faine.'

'Do you want the two of us? Me as a wife and Libby as a mistress?' she asked with bitter scorn.

For a moment the long fingers tightened unbearably on her wrist, then he released it as he said in a shaken voice, 'No. No, of course not.'

'Then I'll go.'

'Very well, then. What will you do?'

Faine smiled, but stopped immediately. While his body had been plundering hers, his lips had exacted another kind of toll, brutally and without tenderness, and her mouth was bruised and sore.

'I'll get a job as a librarian,' she said calmly. 'Don't worry about me.'

'Oh yes, it would be easy for me if I could just cut you out of my life,' he said, suddenly hard. 'I'm not that ruthless, Faine.'

'No, I know.' And because she loved him she said softly, 'It's all right, Burke. Go and get some sleep, you need it.'

She left a week later, two days after they had gone

back to their own house, theirs no longer. Burke had been at home as little as possible; he seemed driven by a force beyond his control. The lines in his face deepened, his expression was that of a man riding himself on a very short rein. Faine was numbed, making arrangements for a new position as far away from Auckland as she could get.

On the morning of her departure she dressed, listening vainly for a sound from the next bedroom. In the end she knocked on the door; Burke called something and she walked in. He was sitting on the edge of his bed, head in his hands.

She stood watching him, remembering the other occasions when he had sat like that. The first time he had demanded and taken the only ease she could give him, the moments of forgetfulness engendered by his pleasure in her body. More than anything she wished now that she could find some way to ease this pain.

He looked up. For a moment the despair in his expression was heartbreakingly revealed, and then the mask came down and he got to his feet, saying wearily, 'You're ready, I gather?'

'Yes.' She came across to him, touched his arm. 'Burke, be happy, *please*!'

Irony touched his smile, but the pale eyes were bleak. 'It's not so simple, is it? Will you be happy?'

'Oh yes.' She managed to smile herself and wondered at the power of the emotion that could summon up such willpower. 'I know you have an over-developed sense of responsibility, but you don't need to worry about me.'

He made as if to say something, then tightened his lips and bent and kissed her cheek. For a horrifying moment her heart threatened to block her throat; she swallowed swiftly and moved away, hanging on to her self-control by a strength of will never possessed before now.

'Keep in touch,' he said harshly, and she nodded, knowing that she wouldn't.

'No, don't come out with me.' She hesitated for a moment, looking at him and then said, 'Goodbye, Burke.'

He said nothing, and she turned and walked away from him while the slow tears clogged her throat and hurt her eyes. They had so nearly made it.

Wellington was warm and sunny with no trace of its notorious winds. Faine stayed there for two nights before taking the Silver Star express back to Auckland and then catching a Road Services bus up to Kaitaia.

Once there she relaxed. Burke would never think of looking for her in the far north and she was almost certain that he had no business interests in this sunny, quiet area cut off by the Maungataniwha Range from the rest of New Zealand. And if he did there was no reason why he should come into the library. It was not as if he would search for her, she thought drearily as she unpacked her bags in the small flat she had managed to rent. Clearly she would be on his conscience for a while, but once he realised that she had deliberately covered her tracks he would be glad to push her to the farthest recesses of his mind. And she had made Ellen promise not to reveal her address when she had been persuaded into writing to her.

After all, he had Libby now. No doubt he would move back with his grandmother so that he could comfort them both.

Strangely enough it was the thought of the house being sold that hurt her most. There were times when she wept at the thought of all of her lovely things being dispersed, the air of serenity and peace disturbed and violated, other unfriendly people dwelling there. Perhaps her patch of violets would waste their sweetness or, worse still, be overgrown once more by greedy oxalis. And would Persephone be again banished to the depths of the shed while a newer, more trendy sculpture took her place?

Of Burke she thought as little as possible, aware that to open the mind to that grief would be unbearable. Later, when she had become used to this feeling of being without half herself, when the single bed she had chosen to sleep in no longer seemed a mutilation, when she had regained her strength, then she would face her loss and grieve for it.

In the meantime she found that superficially her life was pleasant. Her workmates were friendly and open, refusing to allow her to hold herself aloof. They accepted her story of a separation with matter-of-fact sympathy and invited her to their homes, tactfully arranged dates for her and made her smile, teased her about her height and complimented her on her looks and introduced her to the pleasures of life in the far north, from sand yachting at Waipapakauri on the Ninety-Mile Beach, which, she discovered, is only sixty-four miles long, to bush walks. There were treks through the old gumfields at Ahipara and trips up the Aupouri Peninsula to Cape Reinga where the lighthouse shines out over the turbulent meeting place of the Tasman Sea and the Pacific Ocean.

Slowly, very slowly, Faine began to laugh again. The nights were long and hard to bear, but she kept her days pleasantly filled with enough activity to stop her thinking too much.

Winter passed, warm and wet and short, and spring came again; the jonquils and magnolias reminded her so vividly of the time a year ago when she had met Burke that it spoiled her pleasure in the season, but she refused to allow herself to wallow in self-pity. Reluctantly she had begun to face the fact that the love she bore for him was not going to fade and die. Apparently for her there would be no one else who could reach her innermost being, no one whose companionship was so sweet and satisfying.

Well, so be it. She loved him, and because of it she wanted nothing more than for him to be happy. With Libby there was every chance of it. When it stopped hurting so much to think of them together she would be able to accept their happiness without the underlying bitterness which clouded her emotions now.

The flame trees bloomed brilliantly, great orange-scarlet clusters of flowers surrealistic on the bare branches. Beneath the one in her backyard grew freesias, wildlings holding up small white flowers with a purple reverse and the sweetest, most evocative scent in the world. Faine picked bunches of them and put them in vases around her flat, refusing to acknowledge the pain that they caused. She would not allow herself to be crippled by the end of her love affair. Love was supposed to liberate, she told herself sternly; a lost love just as much as a fulfilled one. She would not narrow the pleasures her senses gave her because a scent recalled emotions that had the power to make her heart throb with anguish.

CHAPTER ELEVEN

ONE particularly blustery day Faine went sailing on
Doubtless Bay with a couple who owned a small yacht.
Helen worked in the craft shop next to the library; her
small, wiry husband was involved in forestry. They
made their enjoyment of Faine's company quite obvious and in their undemanding presence she found herself able to relax.

They had left on the tide early in the morning and it
was dark when at last their car drew up outside her
flat. Faine was in shorts, her long golden legs salt-en-
crusted, her hair tumbled with wind and spray.

'A quick shower, then bed,' she said, laughing as she
eased herself out of their battered Mini. 'Thank you
for a lovely day.'

'We'll do it again soon.' Helen grinned. 'Would you
like Greg to see you to the door?'

'This is Kaitaia, not the depths of Auckland. 'Bye,
See you Monday.'

Faine waved goodbye before stooping to pick up the
basket which held the remnants of her lunch and a
change of clothes. The hinge on the gate squeaked
softly as she opened it. The wind had died completely
away and clouds covered the sky, pressing low, heavy
with warm rain. Not one of the neighbouring flats
showed any lights, which was normal for ten o'clock
on a Saturday night. It was very dark.

A tingle of awareness centred between her shoulder
blades made her miss a step. It itched unbearably.

Somewhere in the shadows someone was watching.

Her fingers tightened on the handle of her bag. Without haste she walked up the narrow path, sliding the keys on the keyring until they stuck out between her fingers, forming a crude but effective knuckle-duster. Fear sharpened her senses, but she could see and hear nothing.

Then someone spoke her name and she halted, for a darker piece of shadow detached itself from beside her door and came down the path towards her, and she knew who it was who spoke and who caught her wrist as she lifted her arm.

With the easing of her fear came anger, quick and savage. 'How *dare* you!' she choked, dragging her wrist down to free herself from his grip. 'Just who the *hell* do you think you are, coming here and terrifying the life out of me?'

'Calm down,' he said, and the tolerant, slightly amused tone of his voice fired her anger anew.

But she had recovered some of her poise, enough to know that she must control herself. His touch and his nearness and the dear sound of his voice had sent the long months flying. Gulping, she moved away, furious with herself for having reacted so violently. It took only a moment to insert the key in the lock and go inside. Faine put her bag down in the hall and led the way into her tiny sitting room.

'Oh,' she exclaimed, '*oh*, you *did* give me a fright! Why on earth didn't you let me know you were coming, instead of looming up in the darkness like some—like Jack the Ripper!'

'Mainly because I wasn't sure that I'd find you here if I did.' He was watching her closely, the pale eyes hard and very keen.

'How did you know where I was?' He was here to discuss a divorce, of course he was, so it was stupid to let this wild delight run through her body. Her voice lifted in pitch as she gabbled, 'I suppose you persuaded your grandmother to give it to you. That was unfair— you could have got in touch with me through the lawyer. He——'

'Be quiet,' said Burke, and touched her mouth with his finger, smiling down at her with that totally unfair charm. 'You're thinner,' he went on. 'Why? I don't believe life in Kaitaia is so hectic that you wear yourself to a frazzle trying to cope.' His finger traced a path from her mouth across her determined chin and then down the long line of her throat, finally coming to rest for a moment in the hollow where her heart beat at double speed.

Faine drew a deep breath, forcing herself to return his stare with as much equanimity as she could. Devilish to flirt with her as if the trauma of their marriage didn't lie between them!

'Of course it's not,' she said briskly, moving away from him. 'How did you find my address?'

He grinned, odiously sure of himself. 'From Grandmother, as you guessed. Do you think you could make me a cup of coffee? I'm thirsty.'

'Yes, yes, of course.' She set the percolator going and went back into the sitting room.

Burke was standing by the window looking down at the bowl of freesias. As Faine came into the room he looked up, and something glittered for a moment in the pale gaze before his habitual cool watchfulness hid it. He, too, was thinner. With a pang she realised that not all the suffering had been on her side. But surely, now that Libby was free he should be much more contented, no longer assailed by the corroding hunger she had discerned in him so long ago. For a moment nausea thickened in her throat. Not even to herself would she admit how many of her nights had been spent in sleepless imaginings of him and Libby in each other's arms, locked together in a passion made more profound by their love for each other.

'You look tired,' she blurted. 'Has business been difficult lately?'

Burke smiled somewhat grimly. 'No. Which reminds me—why have you returned the allowance I made you? Poor old Souter rang me up in a great tizz. Very reproachful, he was. I think he fancied you lonely and starving.' His inscrutable glance rested for a moment on her narrow waist and long legs before returning to her face. 'Instead of which you look as though you haven't a care in the world.'

'Mr Souter is a dear,' she retorted, made snappy by the insolence of that swift survey, 'but someone should tell him that in this day and age no one need starve.'

He was watching her with that hooded, deliberate look she knew so well, as though assessing an enemy. He did not have a poker-face; he gave the impression of revealing his thoughts in his features, but it was impossible to tell what went on in that cool, clever brain behind the mask.

'I notice you said nothing about loneliness,' he said now, taking a stem of freesias from the bowl and holding it so that he breathed in the clear, fresh perfume. On any other man the gesture would have been affected, laughable, but somehow Burke managed to make it a formal invitation to confide in him.

Faine shrugged. 'What is there to say? When you go to a new place to live moments of loneliness are inevitable.' She held his gaze defiantly. 'As I'm sure you know. Look, why don't you sit down? How did you get here?'

'Drove up.'

'You must be tired.' She frowned, asking before she lost the courage, 'Why did you come up, Burke? Just to reassure yourself that I'm managing? As you can see, I'm doing fine.'

'Your job?'

'Good. I enjoy it.' She sat down and watched as he lowered himself into the chair opposite her. A thoughtless impulse made her say wryly, 'I don't know how you do it, but you always seem to dwarf everything you ever sit in. You really are huge, aren't you?'

He grinned, lifting an eyebrow at her. 'You make me sound like a mammoth! Why the surprise? You know how big I am.'

A slow painful flush crept from her throat to her forehead. She looked away, unable to face him because he knew what she was thinking, the spark of sensual calculation in his eyes told her that.

'I think the coffee's ready,' she said, and jumped to her feet, moving with less than her usual grace.

Out in her tiny kitchen she stood for a moment breathing deeply, hands clenched on to the stainless steel of the sink-bench, her head bent. Well, she had set herself up for that one, and Burke, being Burke, had let her have it. Of course she knew how big he was! Hadn't she measured him in the most intimate of ways, breast to breast, mouth to mouth, limbs entwined? She knew exactly how heavy he was, how strong he was; she knew the pulse rate of his heart at the moment of agonised ecstasy, she knew—oh, she knew everything about him! She had forgotten nothing. And he knew; it had taken only a fraction of a second for that sexual awareness to glitter in his eyes. You bear my mark, he had said without any need for words, you're branded, and you'll never be free of me.

Faine sighed with shuddering despair, then drew a deep breath and set out pottery mugs on a tray. The coffee was as she liked it, not too strong but rich and fragrant. Back in the sitting room she poured, handed him his mug and said quietly, 'You're up here on business, I take it.'

'No, I came to see you.' He set the untasted mug down on the table by his chair and leaned back, long legs stretched out in front of him, regarding her over the top of his steepled hands with an enigmatic expression.

'A long way to drive when a letter or phone call would have done.'

The broad shoulders lifted slightly. 'Not in this case.' He paused before telling her calmly, 'Libby has gone back to England. For good.'

The coffee was too hot, but Faine drank some just the same. She felt as though she had been hit in the solar plexus—winded and gasping for breath. That was all.

'So?' she said in a cool little voice, looking at the pocket of his shirt.

'So I want you back. And before you explode in righteous indignation,' with a very dry note in the deep voice, 'let me tell you one further thing. I sent her back.'

Her eyes flew to his face, met the same impassive stare. 'Why, Burke? What went wrong?'

'It's very simple. We discovered that whatever we'd had it wasn't love.'

'And how did you discover that?'

A moment's silence before the steady voice told her, 'The usual way.'

Well, she had known. So why did it feel as though she was being stabbed with every breath she took?

But she drank some more of the scalding coffee—tomorrow she would have a sore tongue—and said carefully, 'I'm sorry about that.'

'So am I.'

She could tell from the way Burke spoke that he was smiling and she lifted her lashes and looked at him. The momentary flare of anger died as she saw how totally mirthless that smile was.

'*No!* Sorry that it didn't work out.' And she was sorry for him, but most of all for Libby.

'Are you, Faine?' He spoke quizzically. 'I'd hoped you'd be glad.'

'It doesn't change anything,' she said, tiredness flattening her tones as she stared into the dark depths of the coffee. 'Surely you must see that!'

'No.' His voice was very level, each word cool, remote. 'All I can see is a life without you.'

'Would that be so very bad?'

'It would be the nearest thing to hell this world can offer me.'

Faine looked up, shocked and appalled by the harsh desperation of his voice.

'Burke?' she whispered.

As if his name was the spur to break the immobility of his attitude he got to his feet and came across to kneel beside her, his expression naked and pleading. 'Oh, God, Faine, don't send me away alone,' he said beneath his breath, taking her hand and holding it against his mouth. 'I knew before you left that I was a fool to let you go, but it wasn't until you'd gone that I discovered just how much I need you.'

'Then why——?'

'Why did I let you go?' At her nod he kissed the palm of her hand, and each individual finger, then sat beside her, holding her hands still in his, staring down at them. 'I didn't know,' he said, condemning himself with cold distaste. 'You made it clear that you didn't need me and I felt as though I'd been taken for a ride, falling in love with you when I'd been so sure there would never be anyone else for me but Libby. And she—she'd had no such change of heart. When you left me I felt empty, almost cold, but I was excited.' He lifted a glance of agonised entreaty to her face. 'Must I tell you all this?'

'I think you must,' she said gravely. 'You could fall out of love with me just as easily.'

'So I have to convince you.' He smiled with a hint of his usual dispassionate mockery, but his eyes were afraid.

Faine drew a sharp breath. Burke *afraid*! It seemed a contradiction in terms, that this tough, uncompromising man could feel fear enough to darken the intense colour of his eyes to that of the sea on a stormy day. His jaw was set firmly; he was using all his considerable willpower to maintain his self-control, but a tiny muscle flicked beside his mouth.

'Fair enough,' he said slowly. 'When you left I went back to St Heliers, but I didn't sell our house. I told myself that the emptiness I felt was because you'd been such a good companion. And I can't deny that——' he paused before saying thickly, 'I'd wanted her for so long. It came as a hell of a shock when I realised that she meant no more to me than most of the others. I liked her and when I touched her I pretended she was you. I know that makes me a swine.' His fingers tightened cruelly on hers, preventing her instinctive withdrawal. 'Listen to me,' he said half under his breath. 'Please, listen to me. We didn't make love. We tried—but I was unable to.'

Faine hadn't been able to hide her revulsion at his words, but there was no resisting the appeal in his voice. He looked almost ill, pale beneath his tan, skin stretched tightly over the hard framework of his face, a white line around his mouth.

Without thought she twisted her hands to enfold him in a warm clasp. 'It doesn't matter,' she said quietly. 'Darling, it doesn't matter.'

'Yes, it does. It matters. I know that I've behaved despicably, and I know that, God knows why, you love me in spite of it.' He gave her a twisted smile as the shock registered in her expression. 'I had my suspicions when you left, but I wasn't certain until I saw you again. For a moment you came out from behind that cool façade and I saw the real you, the person you kept so well hidden from me even when we made love.' He lifted his hands and kissed her wrists where the small blue vein throbbed its unmistakable message. 'Oh, God, my heart,' he muttered thickly, his voice rough with desire, 'I've craved for you, hungered for you, thirsted for you, *ached* for you, night after night, day after day, and known that I'd treated you damnably and Libby worse. I couldn't bear to touch her and she knew it—and knew why.'

'She *knew*?' Faine felt herself go cold. 'How?'

'She's not stupid,' he said drily. 'Things became tense and strained—inevitably we had a row. She flung her suspicions at me, so I told her the truth.' A lean finger touched Faine's mouth, stopping the impetuous flow of words. Wearily he continued, 'I did love her, in a way. Not as I love you—but she was gallant and loyal, and Gavin behaved like a swine to her. She tried so hard to hide her unhappiness—sometimes she looked like a lost kid, afraid that she'd never be found. I felt so bloody sorry for her. And she is beautiful, I couldn't help wanting her. Then you came along and I thought it would make things easier for everyone if I married, remove the temptation for both of us. The way things were sooner or later we'd have slept together, and she couldn't handle any more guilt.'

A jagged spear of jealousy tore through Faine's body. She knew she lost colour, knew that Burke recognised it for what it was; she could see understanding in his glance, but his voice remained detached.

'Well, it effectively removed any temptation for me to stray,' he went on evenly. 'I found you desirable right from the start. What I didn't realise was that as my hunger for you increased my feelings for Libby decreased. I deliberately pushed her to the back of my mind. It wasn't hard. As well as being extremely sexy you were a terrific companion, intelligent, compassionate, funny and sweet and opinionated. I suppose I must have started to fall in love with you right at the beginning. I hated seeing you with anyone else. That night at the Yacht Club—that was when I made up my mind that I was going to have you. But you are a very cool lady. You fascinated and intrigued me.'

'So you tilted at my equilibrium every chance you got.' Her expression was wry yet understanding. A hard man, with a hard analytical brain, it had amused him to try to tip her off balance, amused him and perhaps satisfied that instinct for domination which lay beneath the sophisticated mask the world saw.

'Yes.' The pale eyes blazed for a moment. 'I enjoyed it, but it irritated me that you had enough strength of will not to cave in. You responded very satisfactorily to my lovemaking, but I wanted to see you helpless, completely at my mercy. And I still didn't know why. You never completely capitulated, did you, darling? I knew that there was this core of steel. I admired it but wanted to shatter it. It showed so clearly after you'd seen Libby and me together. No recriminations, no tears, although it was obvious that you'd had one hell of a shock.' His hand touched her mouth gently, tracing the shape of it, then he caught her to him, holding her so tightly that it hurt to breathe. Thickly, half hesitant, he muttered, 'Oh God, I love you! And I don't deserve you, but I'll never let you go now.'

Faine could feel the tension and excitement building in him, knew a wild response, but dampened it with a deliberation born of months of self-discipline. Before she gave herself wholly she must know, for certain.

'You wouldn't let me go then,' she said in muffled tones into his chest.

The crushing hold relaxed. 'I suppose my subconscious knew,' he agreed, pushing up her chin so that he could see her flushed face. His mouth swooped, kissed her eyelids closed and he added with a note of self-derision, 'Of course, the fact that I was certain that you'd surrender within a few weeks could have had something to do with it. But you held out—charming, friendly, and so bloody self-possessed that I felt like smashing furniture every time I left you at your bedroom door.' He laughed on a note of irony. 'You put me through hoops and I didn't know what the hell was happening to me. When Gavin and Libby came to dinner that night I was almost at the end of my tether. You seemed like a star, warm and golden and glowing, and just as unattainable. Libby was a mass of nerves, Gavin was—well, you remember how he was. When they left I walked the floor, almost convincing myself that I hated you. I had to leave before you woke the next morning, otherwise I'd have taken you. I hoped you'd be asleep when I got home. I told myself that all I needed was time to cool down. Then you came in and—well, everything came together.'

Faine touched her hand to his, holding it still against her breast. The memories of that night were still so vivid that colour flamed in her cheeks, and Burke laughed, very sure of himself now.

'It was a revelation,' he told her, the pale eyes teasing, warm with memories. 'You blew my mind. I couldn't believe that you could be a virgin and yet respond so passionately. I was so bloody arrogant that I gloated at the thought that I'd been the first, that there would be no other man for you. And then Gavin died.'

'I couldn't take it in,' she said, her voice very low. 'That day I hoped that perhaps you were beginning to love me. But when I walked into the hospital you were holding Libby and I saw your face, and I knew that it had been wishful thinking. I couldn't—I think I died inside.'

'I'm sorry,' Burke said harshly, holding her close. 'So sorry. It means nothing, I know, but if I could have saved you a moment's pain I'd have cut an arm off. But she—she needed me and, God help me, I mistook the compassion I felt for love.'

She believed him now. 'It doesn't matter. Burke, it doesn't matter any more.'

'No.' His arms tightened around her. For long moments he held her against his chest, his cheek resting on the amber curls. Faine slid her hands across his back, while a great peace enveloped her. For the first time since her parents died she felt safe. It had taken them a long time to reach this haven, many misunderstandings to be rectified, much soul-searching and the recognition of emotions for what they really were, but at last they had got there.

'Gavin suspected,' said Burke, his voice muffled in her hair. 'Our marriage lulled his suspicions. He liked you immensely; I think it amused him that I'd married someone who didn't hang on my every word. He was always inclined to be a bit jealous of me, though God knows why.'

Faine lifted her head, eyes laughing. 'You don't really mean that!' she exclaimed, teasing him in return.

He grinned, not altogether without cynicism.

'Had he been the one with the money he'd have had just as much luck.'

Incredibly enough, he meant it. Very gently Faine kissed the hard line of his jaw. 'Darling, you don't really believe that.'

'Convince me.'

She laughed but shook her head. 'Not yet. You thought I'd married you for your money, didn't you?'

'No, not the money. I thought you wanted the sort of life I could give you, the security that my money represented. It seemed perfectly logical. Your parents' deaths and your fiancé's rejection had shattered your world, left you almost entirely alone.' His hooded gaze rested for a long moment on the generous curves of her mouth, the smooth line of cheek and jaw, then a deep note of anger roughened his voice. 'When I made mild love to you your reaction delighted me, although I was always aware that in spite of your warmth and that passionate response you couldn't hide, you were holding back. I thought you'd surrender completely when we slept together, but although you were everything a man could want there was still that aloofness. Physically you gave me everything I asked——'

'And resented you for being able to reduce me to such a state,' she interrupted, able now to tell him.

'I know.' His grin was smug, extremely self-satisfied, but it faded as he continued quietly, 'Even when you were lost in my arms I knew that some part of you was an onlooker. You were in command. I suppose I wanted you to love me and be unable to hide it. When you kept silent it infuriated me. I think that was why I raped you after the funeral.'

As if impelled by his memories he released her and walked across to the window, staring out with an intentness that almost convinced her that he could see through the thick darkness outside.

'I was glad to see you go,' the even voice went on mercilessly. 'I turned to Libby eagerly, even then not realising that I was using her to banish your image. It didn't take her long to discover it, however. When we had that row she told me that I was in love with you.'

He smiled, coldly cynical, a bitter movement without amusement. 'It took me a while to accept it, but in my heart I knew she was right. Finally we sat down and talked it out, and she decided to go back home.'

Faine made a soft sound of protest, but instinct prevented the words from tumbling forth. After a moment Burke turned and looked at her, heavy lids hiding any emotion.

'Not a pleasant interview,' he said roughly. 'But I wasn't going to make another mistake. For a man who'd thought himself comparatively sophisticated I'd made more than enough. The biggest one was thinking that what I felt for you was only affection flavoured with lust. Do you think you can forgive me for that, Faine?'

He looked directly at her, his eyes revealing a naked appeal stripped of everything but the starkness of his need.

'You know the answer to that,' she told him as she got to her feet and went across to him, sliding her arms around him to hold him close against her.

'I don't deserve you,' he whispered shakily, 'but I love you, love you, love you beyond all hope, all reason, all desire.' His hands framed her face, the strong fingers trembling. 'You're so beautiful,' he said, his gaze moving restlessly over her features. 'Strong and beautiful and kind, and there hasn't been a minute since I met you that I haven't thought of you.'

'I thought you were a man who never exaggerated,' she said, smiling because if she didn't she would weep. Turning her head, she kissed the palm of his hand. 'I love you—I have since the second time we met. You kissed me and I wanted you, and then you laughed and my heart melted. I didn't know what had happened to me, but I realised that for my peace of mind I'd better not see any more of you. Nothing like it had ever happened before.'

'Not even with that fool you were engaged to?' Burke demanded quickly, jealously.

'Dougal? Oh no. I tried to convince myself that it was just that I fancied you like mad, but when I found myself agreeing to marry you I realised that it had to be love. I knew you weren't in love with me, you see.'

His fingers tightened hurtfully, then he smiled and the pale depths of his eyes warmed. 'The fact that I hated to think of you with a *fiancé* should have warned me that I was in too deep to climb out,' he said huskily. 'I'd never cared before, not even with Libby, but the thought of you making love with anyone else but me bothered me so much that I pushed it out of my mind.' He grinned and bent and kissed her, then kissed her again, not at all gently, and bit the lobe of her ear before whispering, 'I suppose it's too much to hope that this place has a double bed in it?'

'Well, no, but the bed is a very large single,' she said demurely, then, 'Burke!'

For he bent and lifting her as easily as if she were a child, shouldered his way through the door into the tiny passage and from thence to the bedroom, finding his way by instinct, so Faine told him.

'Perhaps, but I was never as licentious as you seem to think.' He dropped her on to the bed and stood looking down at her, a hot tide of emotion running between them. Speaking slowly, deliberately, he added, 'Does my past bother you?'

She shook her head, her love so blatant in the warm depths of her eyes that he drew in a deep sharp breath and knelt to put his mouth against the warm swell of her breast.

Even through the thin cotton of her shirt the heat of his lips woke something deep and primeval with Faine. She ran her hand the length of his body, felt the muscles harden beneath her touch and without any hesitation pulled his shirt open so that she could explore his body more easily.

'Darling,' he muttered against her skin, regaining

the initiative with a swift movement which deprived her of her shirt. He smiled, that set, humourless movement of his mouth which she had remembered so often in the long reaches of the night, and revealed some of his experience in the ease with which he got rid of the rest of her clothes.

For a long moment he looked at her, his gaze feasting on the soft blush that coloured her skin. Then he said in a voice thick and hoarse with desire, 'Dear God, you are so beautiful.'

'So are you,' she said, knowing that she was not beautiful and so thankful that to his eyes she was fairer than any other woman on earth that her lips trembled. 'Oh, I've missed you,' she said, her voice a thread of sound in the quiet room. 'I've missed you so, my darling.'

'I'll never let you go again,' he promised before his hands and mouth stirred her to a desire so ravenous that she couldn't wait for the long, slow arousal he had seduced her with before. Almost angrily she pulled him into her, accepting the sudden driving invasion of his body with a fierce response as though they fought each other in a battle which could have only one ending. Burke said something, asked something, but the wild clamour of her heart deafened her and she moaned, 'Please—oh, please . . .' and then cried out as the rapture exploded within her and together they came home to that place she had once thought unattainable.

A long time after, when she had showered and slept and woken again and woken him and they were lying once more locked together in the languid aftermath of passion, Burke said exultantly, 'I love you. I love you when you behave like a wanton in my arms, totally without inhibitions, and I love you when you lose your

temper with me and I loved you when I came home
one evening and found you pulling oxalis leaves out of
those wretched violets when you should have been getting me some sort of meal.' His arms tightened. 'And
now that I've got you I'm never going to let you go.
This is a life sentence, dear heart. Think you can cope?'

'Oh, I'm sure I can,' she said with such complete
conviction that he laughed and kissed her hair and said,
'Well, if that's so, let's get some more sleep. We've all
our lives ahead of us.'

CHAPTER TWELVE

'ARE you *sure* you want to come out to the airport with
me?'

Faine sighed theatrically. 'Darling *idiot* husband, of
course I do! Being pregnant doesn't automatically
qualify me for a wheelchair, you know!'

Burke smiled, but there was a look in his pale eyes
which made her get swiftly to her feet.

'Things which could have been better said,' she
groaned as she went into his arms. 'Darling, let Gavin
rest in peace.'

'When I see Libby I'll be able to,' he said, kissing
her forehead, closing each eye with a further kiss and
from there moving to her mouth.

Some time later she broke, flushed and heavy-eyed,
from his arms. 'And that had better be enough to that!
Or we'll never get there on time. It's not fashionable
for a man to be so besotted by his wife after two years
of marriage.'

Burke grinned with lazy insolence and pulled her back into his arms, bending his head to kiss the length of her throat while one hand rested on the thickened waistline which was so far the only sign of her pregnancy.

'I like making you look like that,' he taunted, then, suddenly serious as she buried her face into his shoulder, 'Only you, my dearest. I wonder why you're the only woman who's left me constantly unsated, always yearning for more.'

Faine muttered something into the hard muscle, felt it flex against her cheek, and then he said quietly, 'Because what I feel for you is so much more than desire, I suppose, although I must admit that's a very pleasant part of our life together. You've given me so much, Faine. Thank you.'

'For loving you?' Unbearably moved, she rubbed her brow against him. 'Stupid man, as if I could help it! I could no more stop loving you than I could stop breathing.'

She lifted her head, met the warm tenderness of his glance, the tenderness which only she ever saw, and smiled mistily up at him. 'I do love you. I always will.'

'I hope to God that Libby feels the same about her man,' he said, adding with self-mockery, 'and then perhaps I'll be able to relax and fully accept this most unexpected happiness.'

Faine nodded, knowing that he still felt a keen responsibility for Libby. As she turned so that he could slip a coat over her shoulders, for the evenings were still cool, she found herself hoping fervently that Libby's marriage was as firmly based as theirs. Two months ago Libby had written to Ellen to tell her that she intended to marry one Ralph Somerville, an artist whose name was well-known enough to be recognised even twelve thousand miles away.

Ever since then Faine had kept her fingers crossed for her. So happy herself that she could not imagine a greater happiness, she wished the same for Libby, knowing that Burke still felt guilty about his treatment of her. Now Libby and her husband were almost here, and for different reasons everyone was a little tense about the visit.

One glance at Libby's face as she came through the doors at the airport reassured them all, for she was radiant, gazing adoringly up at the tall, thin man beside her as she presented him with a quiet confidence which spoke volumes. Libby had at last found a man she could rely on.

'That's what I wanted,' she confided, later that evening as she and Faine walked in the cool air on the terrace of the St Heliers house. The lights along the Waterfront Drive glowed below them like an illuminated necklace around the broad sweep of the harbour. Across the dark water the long peninsula of the North Shore was another mass of lights and against the sky the conical bulk of Rangitoto, the Island of the Bleeding Sky, loomed in heavy primeval darkness.

'I fell for Gavin like a ton of bricks,' Libby continued, staring into the darkness. 'It was sheer physical attraction. Even before the accident it was wearing thin. I wanted children, a home, and he didn't. But of course once he was hurt I couldn't leave him.' She glanced across at Faine, as though hesitant. 'And Burke—well, he was everything Gavin was not. Strong and totally dependable, masterful without being cruel—I felt so *secure* with him.' Libby sighed. 'I wouldn't be telling you this, but I want the past over and done with. And so do you I think.'

'Yes. It—Burke still feels a heel over letting you down.'

'Lord, he didn't let me down.' Libby laughed softly. 'You know, looking back, I can't even begin to understand how I felt about him. I think I must have been in such a state of shock while I lived here that I didn't know what I was doing half the time. I leaned shamelessly on Burke while Gavin was alive, using his strength and his integrity as a prop. When you were married I felt totally bereft, as though he'd deserted me.' She stooped, picked a sprig of white alyssum from between the flagstones and smelt it. 'Mmm, lovely, like warm honey. And of course he has that terrific sexual magnetism . . . A pretty explosive combination! When Gavin died I was lost. I felt so guilty, as though Burke and I had killed him. Then you left and he came back and I wanted the warmth of a relationship—any kind of relationship would have done, I think. Did he tell you what happened?'

Faine hesitated, then said frankly, 'Not exactly, no. That you and he—that you'd tried to make love, yes. But only that he didn't—he couldn't.'

Of the two she was the more embarrassed. Libby laughed again and put a warm hand over Faine's, squeezing hard for a moment before releasing her, saying, 'He was madly in love with you, of course. Even in my peculiar state that impinged. I was furious. But I had a few remnants of sense left. We had a terrific fight—God, he frightened me, he went all cold and viciously sarcastic—well, he must have done some hard thinking and sorting out, because some days later we had a talk. He pointed out how futile the whole situation was and that he was going to see if you'd have him back and what did I plan to do? I said I'd go back home. And,' she said more strongly, 'it was the best thing I ever did. Did you know he supported me? What I'd felt for Burke was a kind of reversion back to childhood with sexual overtones. I needed to have someone to rely on, someone stronger to kiss me better and tell me that everything was going to be fine. Even Burke must have known that what was between us wasn't really love, or he'd never have thought of marrying you.'

'I suppose not,' Faine said quietly.

'I *know* not!' Libby was emphatic, the clipped English voice clear on the night air. 'I mean, can you *imagine* marrying anyone else now, feeling the way you do about Burke?' She laughed at Faine's vigorous head shake and said dreamily, 'Nor me. Ralph is everything I've ever wanted, so thoughtful and exciting to be with, and it turns me on just to look at him.'

'Thanks for the recommendation.' Her husband had come up behind them and put an arm around his wife's waist, pulling her back against him. Above Libby's head, resting gracefully on his shoulder, he said, 'Ghosts laid?'

'Yes, darling.'

'Good. Let's go in. I thought this part of New Zealand was subtropical! That's a chilly breeze.'

Libby returned some laughing answer and they all three went back into the house where Ellen and Burke waited.

Later that evening in their bedroom Faine sat up against the pillows and drank hot milk and told Burke what Libby had said, her expression a little remote.

'Don't,' he said, taking her beaker and setting it on the bedside table so that he could sit down on the edge of the bed.

'Don't what?' She was surprised and showed it.

He took her hands and held them against his cheek. 'Don't go away from me. You used to look like that when first we were married and I felt as though you'd shut me out completely.' He lifted her hands, kissed the palm of each with sensuous enjoyment, his tongue lingering on the fine skin. 'Fool that I was, I didn't know why I hated it, but I did.'

Desire, familiar yet ever-fresh, strong with sweet certitude between them. 'Happy now?' Faine asked huskily, her love so apparent in her expression that he drew a sharp breath.

'Yes.' He slid the soft silk of her nightgown from her shoulders, his expression intent and devouring. 'I'm glad Libby has found what she wanted. Have I told you that being pregnant suits you?'

His hands touched the sensitive skin of her breasts, tracing their outline with a gentleness which inflamed her.

'No jealousy?' she probed.

Burke laughed beneath his breath and bent his head to kiss the pale skin his seeking hands had exposed. 'Only when Ralph claimed relationship and kissed you. Then I felt jealous.' For a moment his mouth was ruthless, the kiss marking the skin. 'I don't like any other man to touch you. You're mine, heart, body and soul.' He looked at her with the kind of passionate love she had never hoped to see in his eyes. 'I'll let you keep ownership of your mind, but everything else is mine.'

Leaning forward, Faine slid her hand across the

smooth skin of his shoulders, enjoying the swift hardening of his muscles at her touch. Set free of her inhibitions by his ardent delight in her body, she revelled in the knowledge that she could make his heart thunder beneath her fingers. Their mutual passion was a rare and delightful thing, but even more important was the complete trust that had evolved between them.

She said so, and he smiled and kissed her and slid his arms beneath her shoulders, saying wickedly, 'More important? You think so now, but try telling me that in—let's say, twenty minutes' time? You're as sensual as you're kindhearted, my heart, and I don't know which I love most.' For a moment his mouth hardened, then he bent his head and whispered, 'Love me. Love me as I love you. With all that I am, all that I can be.'

The unhidden need in his voice called forth a similar response from her. 'Always,' she said, the word a vow, before she surrendered to the hunger and strength of their passion, confident that their love would endure any test brought against it.

Harlequin Plus
A WORD ABOUT THE AUTHOR

Robyn Donald cannot remember ever being unable to read. She learned the skill at a very early age; and today, she claims, reading remains one of her great pleasures, "if not a vice."

Robyn, her husband and their two children make their home in a small country village in the historic Bay of Islands in the far north of New Zealand. Both the climate and the people are friendly, and her family enjoys sailing in particular and the outdoor life in general.

Her other interests include cooking, music and astronomy. And she finds history and archaeology especially fascinating because "they are about the sum total of human experience."

When she writes, Robyn visualizes scenes that she knows and loves. The actual germ of a story arrives "ready-made from some recess of my brain, but," she adds, "it takes quite a while to work out the details!"

Take these
4 best-selling novels
FREE

Yes! Four sophisticated, contemporary love stories by four world-famous authors of romance FREE, as your introduction to the Harlequin Presents subscription plan. Thrill to **Anne Mather**'s passionate story BORN OUT OF LOVE, set in the Caribbean.... Travel to darkest Africa in **Violet Winspear**'s TIME OF THE TEMPTRESS....Let **Charlotte Lamb** take you to the fascinating world of London's Fleet Street in MAN'S WORLD .... Discover beautiful Greece in **Sally Wentworth**'s moving romance SAY HELLO TO YESTERDAY.

Harlequin Presents...

The very finest in romance fiction

Join the millions of avid Harlequin readers all over the world who delight in the magic of a really exciting novel. EIGHT great NEW titles published EACH MONTH! Each month you will get to know exciting, interesting, true-to-life people .... You'll be swept to distant lands you've dreamed of visiting .... Intrigue, adventure, romance, and the destiny of many lives will thrill you through each Harlequin Presents novel.

Get all the latest books before they're sold out!
As a Harlequin subscriber you actually receive your personal copies of the latest Presents novels immediately after they come off the press, so you're sure of getting all 8 each month.

Cancel your subscription whenever you wish!
You don't have to buy any minimum number of books. Whenever you decide to stop your subscription just let us know and we'll cancel all further shipments.